THE THIRD MUSKETEER

by

James I. McArthur

PublishAmerica
Baltimore

© 2010 by James I. McArthur.
All rights reserved. No part of this book may be reproduced, stored in a retrieval system or transmitted in any form or by any means without the prior written permission of the publishers, except by a reviewer who may quote brief passages in a review to be printed in a newspaper, magazine or journal.

First printing

All characters in this book are fictitious, and any resemblance to real persons, living or dead, is coincidental.

PublishAmerica has allowed this work to remain exactly as the author intended, verbatim, without editorial input.

ISBN: 978-1-61582-882-1 (softcover)
ISBN: 978-1-4489-9211-9 (hardcover)
PUBLISHED BY PUBLISHAMERICA, LLLP
www.publishamerica.com
Baltimore

Printed in the United States of America

PROLOGUE

The soldiers appeared tall and gaunt as they struggled across the rugged terrain, which was covered with dwarf juniper bushes. Their faces reflected the exhaustion and fatigue they felt within, while their ponchos blew in the silent wind. Each had an obstacle before him that had to be overcome. But even with their weariness, they were alert and ready for danger as they proceeded on patrol.

Upon closer inspection one could see that the men were not all soldiers—some were sailors, marines, air force pilots—in fact every branch of military service was represented among the 19 men pushing across the hill side. Also, as one studied their thin and tired faces, every ethnic group was present in the patrol.

These men were not real, but they did represent real American heroes. These men were statues, a tribute to the 54,000 American men and women who gave their lives in the Korean War. Most visitors to this stirring memorial in the Washington National Mall were emotionally moved by the tribute, and many, especially veterans from the conflict, were often openly in tears. Over 2 ½ million visitors had visited the memorial the previous year. Today the mall was crowded with summer tourists.

One man, however, in a business suit and carrying a brief case, seemed unmoved by the graphic scene. He studied the figures for a few minutes and then proceeded to a bench by the adjacent Pool of Remembrance. It was a quiet place intended for reflection, with a granite slab listing the numbers killed, missing in action and wounded in the war. An inscription on the wall read:

"Our nation honors her sons and daughters who answered the call to defend a country they never knew and a people they never met."

The man rested on the bench, pushing his brief case well under the seat. He lit a cigarette and studied the crowd for a while, until he was sure that all the people who had been there when he first sat down had moved on. Now a new group of spectators was slowly passing by, studying the monument to the men and women who had fought for freedom for a country in a distant part of the world.

The man got up, snuffed out his cigarette, and strode purposely to Independence Avenue, and then down West Basin Drive to the Franklin D. Roosevelt Memorial. He was relieved that there were no shouts from anyone in the crowd telling him that he was forgetting his brief case. When he reached the entrance to the FDR Memorial he paused, pulled a cell phone from his pocket and punched in a few numbers.

Within seconds there was a deafening explosion at the bench he had just left. The man smiled briefly and pocketed his cell phone. "Now it is Fatim and Mullah's turn," he muttered to himself.

As if on cue there was another explosion, this time at the center of the great wall of the Vietnam Memorial. And then a third blast at the Rainbow Pool of the newly dedicated WWII Memorial in front of the Washington Monument.

Allah is great, the man thought with a wry smile, as he turned and walked away from the confused and terrified crowds of people, some rushing towards the locations of the blasts and others moving swiftly away.

Over 50 tourists were killed in the three explosions, with many more injured, and the nation's three great tributes to American men and women who had fought against injustice and tyranny in the world in the 20th century, had been badly damaged.

CHAPTER ONE

The train slowed perceptively as it neared the center of the small Midwestern town in central Kansas. Ben Foxworth leaned forward in his seat and gazed at the houses passing slowly past his window, shining brightly in the twilight sun. He unexpectedly felt an overwhelming sense of nostalgia.

The homes were all distinct, but Ben thought they still had a sameness about them, that could only be found in a small town such as this. Although they were of different shapes and style, they were lined up on the block in a row, as if the front of each house had been carefully measured from the street. Each had a green lawn in the front yard which was divided into four squares by sidewalks; one running the length of the block about 10 feet in from the curb, and another leading from the front of each house, intersecting the block-long sidewalk, and continuing on to the street.

Nearly all the houses had white shingle siding, and all had a large front porch looking out on the street. They were well maintained, and the lawns were freshly mowed. Very few had patios of any sort in the rear, although all had a large grassy back yard. Many had gardens. At the rear of each lot ran the alley, dividing these homes from the row of homes on the next street.

This was the town in which Ben had grown up, and now as he looked out at the passing scene, he was overwhelmed with a flood of memories. He remembered playing in these yards and visiting with friendly neighbors. One of these was Mrs. Brown, who lived next door to their home, who always had freshly baked cookies which she liked to share with the kids in the neighborhood. Ben could almost smell the aroma from these delicacies even now.

This led to other recollections, of high school football games, dances, other school activities, and of course fishing trips and duck hunting with his close friends, Buddy Callahan and John Wilkerson. John's father had belonged to a local sportsmen club, and the three high school chums had spent many a freezing winter's morning hiding out in a duck blind waiting for the mallards to fly in to the pond. Ben smiled as he remembered what a hard time they always had of keeping Buddy from jumping up and shooting before the other two were ready. They always said they would fire on the count of three, but Buddy, greatly excited, would leap up and blast away at the count of two and a half.

Ben Foxworth, 68 years old, was coming back to his home town for the 50th high school reunion of his class. He didn't look like a man nearing his seventies—average height, strong features, dark hair and a limber body. His grey eyes shone with a youthful sparkle, and his wide mouth was most often turned up in a friendly smile. He still wasn't quite sure why he had decided to come back for the reunion since he had not attended any of them since the 5th so many years ago, and had not kept in touch with any of his old school mates. *Probably because I'm bored and at loose ends,* he thought, *and this seemed like something to do.*

Ben leaned back in his seat as another set of memories swept over him. Memories of Mary, his wife of 45 years, and the happiness they shared, and then of the battle they had waged together over the past year with her cancer. As stressful as these past months had been for the both of them, it had also brought them even closer together, if that was possible. When his wife died, it left a great vacuum in his life. And a great anger at how unfair life was. An anger that he couldn't seem to shake. Ben had few hobbies or interests outside of their marriage, and now time lay heavily on his days.

His daughter, Beth, lived in Seattle with her husband and child. He loved them dearly but they were far away and busy with their own lives. Beth, however, was currently on a campaign to get Ben to move closer to them.

He and Mary had many friends in Colorado, but now that Mary was gone, he felt somewhat estranged from the couples they had enjoyed together. When they invited him for dinner or cocktails, it was not the same as when Mary was by his side.

With a start Ben realized that the train had stopped, and passengers were readying themselves for departure. The conductor came through the coach informing everyone that they had arrived at Oldvil, Kansas, and that they would be here for 20 minutes.

Ben gathered up his bags and stepped off the train. In front of him was the old Santa Fe depot. Once again he experienced a flood of memories about a building that had been a central gathering place for their town, a place where friends and family were either leaving or coming back—a place that experienced both joys and sadness. Ben vaguely remembered during World War II that the churches had set up a canteen in the depot, serving cookies and hot chocolate to the soldiers passing through on troop trains. His mother had been one of the leaders in the effort.

The building still looked exactly as he remembered it on the outside, but once inside he realized that the depot area itself was greatly reduced in size from its former grandeur. Now much of the building had been converted to office space—insurance agents and lawyers, he noted. The depot area itself was very small. This struck Ben as sad.

He approached the ticket counter, identified himself, and asked if the keys for a rental car had been left for him. The clerk smiled, reached under the counter, and produced an envelope with Ben's name on it. He handed it to Ben without asking for identification.

Ben thanked him and retrieved the packet. *One of the wonders of a small town*, he thought. *Just call up the car rental company and ask them to leave the keys at the ticket counter. It's a place where people still trust each other and take each other at their word.* He tried to imagine this happening in a big city, like Chicago, but without much luck. Of course in Chicago, the rental company would be located at the depot anyway.

Ben found his car, and then, although it was now around 9:00 p.m., decided to cruise down the main street of the town before heading to his motel. This of course didn't take long.

The main street looked exactly as he remembered it. Many of the stores had changed names, but the old drug store where he had worked in high school was still there. And there was the Handley Shoe Store, same as ever. And the book store where he had bought most of his school books—the music store was still there—a new Greek restaurant—the old court house—J. C. Penny's was gone, but there was another clothing store in its place.

The old town hasn't changed that much, Ben thought. This gave him a great deal of comfort. *Guess the shopping malls and Wal-Mart must be out on the edge of town. Well, that's a good place for them. Need to just keep them there.*

With that thought in mind, Ben drove to the outskirts of town and located the motel where the reunion was being held, which sure enough was located near a Wal-Mart. The motel was a large, modern, two-story building with a dining room, a bar and an indoor swimming pool.

The clerk produced a layout of the motel and showed Ben how to find his room. It was in the rear of the motel on the first floor. All of the rooms opened to an inside corridor. Entrances to the corridor were through the front office, or through secured entry ways half way back and in the rear. In Ben's case, the best entrance was in the rear, so he returned to the car and drove to the back of the motel.

Nothing like this when I was growing up here, Ben thought, as he entered the building and found his room. *And we even have air conditioning.*

Ben unpacked his suitcase, remembering hot, summer nights when he was growing up, when he would lay on his bed, stripped to his shorts, hoping for a breeze through the open window. He also remembered the lonely night-call of trains as they announced their approach into the town. It was a haunting and lonely sound which pierced the stillness of the night.

For the first time in months Ben felt the slow anger that was always with him begin to dissipate just a little. Anger at having lost Mary at the time of life that they should have been enjoying it the most.

Ben forced his thoughts back to his high school days. As he did so he felt himself relaxing once again. *Memories of youth when times seemed simple and hopes soared to the sky,* he thought as he drifted off to sleep. *Aren't they wonderful?*

CHAPTER TWO

The next morning Ben rose early, showered and shaved, and went for a short walk on the sidewalk in front of the motel. The morning air was brisk, but promised to warm up into one of those late-summer hot days. The birds seemed to enjoy the cool air, chattering sharply in the large cottonwood trees.

He returned to the motel and entered the restaurant for breakfast. There was a scattering of people at the tables and in the booths, and Ben looked sharply at each group, trying to decide if it might be some of his old classmates.

The reunion didn't officially start till the next night, Friday, with a barbecue at the athletic park, followed by a high school football game. The banquet itself was scheduled for Saturday night. But tonight a cocktail party was being hosted by one of the locals for any of the early-comers, and Ben decided that this would provide a good opportunity to get reacquainted with his old school chums.

At one of the tables in the back of the room Ben saw four men about his age in animated conversation. He looked them over carefully, and thought he might know one of them. *What was his name—Tom—Tom Adams was it?*

While Ben searched his memory, the man he thought might be Tom was studying him with equal intensity. The man got up, came over to Ben, and said, "You're Ben Foxworth aren't you? I'm Tom Aldrich." Without waiting for a reply, he shook Ben's hand, and turning to the others at the table announced in a loud voice," Hey, guys, it's old Ben Foxworth himself, back for the reunion."

The others got up from the table and shook Ben's hand, introducing themselves. Ben vaguely remembered the names of the first two, but had a hard time putting any kind of face to them. Then the fourth man, whose back had been to Ben, turned around and with a big grin, came over and gave Ben a big bear hug.

""Buddy Callahan," Ben exploded. "My God, it's been a long time. I was hoping you would be here." Ben stood back and looked at his old friend. "You look in pretty good shape for an old man."

"And so do you, Ben," Buddy replied. "It's good to see you. I was afraid there might not be anyone here from our old gang. Come on, sit down and tell me what's been going on in your life."

Buddy Callahan and Ben, along with John Wilkerson, had been almost inseparable in high school. The three had played football, basketball and been in high school drama groups, and almost always double or triple dated for movies, proms or other social gatherings.

For the next hour, over several coffees, the men exchanged stories of the long forgotten past—of trouble they had been in at school, of championship basketball tournaments, of pranks they had played on each other and their teachers. Ben marveled at how some of them could remember these incidents with such vivid clarity, while to him many of the exploits barely rang a bell.

"So what do you do all alone up there in your mountains all day?" Buddy asked Ben.

"Oh I'm not alone. I have Sadie to keep me company. She and I play around quite a bit."

Buddy gave Ben a quizzical look. "Sadie? Well fancy that. You've been holding out on me."

"Well, you and I haven't seen each other for quite a few years. I didn't see any reason to rush right into my social life. Sadie and I have been a pair for several years now," Ben said with a twinkle in his eye.

"Several years? And Mary just passed on this past year?"

"Yes. But not to worry. Mary loved Sadie as much as I do."

This was almost too much for Buddy. Ben finally took pity on him and said, "Sadie is my dog. A full grown Lab Retriever. I don't know what I'd do without her to keep me company."

Buddy heaved a sigh of relief. "For a minute there I was beginning to wonder about you."

During a lull in the conversation they looked up to see three women enter the restaurant and take a seat at the far side of the room.

"Hey, that's April Showers and Ann Darsey," one of the men observed. "Don't know the other one. April's the one giving the cocktail party tonight."

Ben looked up with a new interest. *Ann Darsey*, he thought. He suddenly realized that he had been hoping she might be here, that he would like to see her again.

Ben and Ann had been a pair in high school. They had "gone steady" during their junior and senior years, and everyone had assumed they would get married shortly after graduation. But Ben had gone away to a college back east to study pre-law, and she had gone to a junior college near their hometown. At first during their separation they had written to each other almost daily, then it had tapered off to weekly, and then even less often. They got together during school holidays, and once Ann had come back to Ben's school for a formal dance, but gradually they drifted further apart.

One day Ben received a letter from Ann stating that she had met someone very special, and that they were going to be married. For some reason, this hadn't upset Ben nearly as much as he thought it should. He had moved on to a different world and had left high school memories far behind.

Then he met Mary, and whatever misgivings he might have had about Ann vanished completely. He and Mary were married after a quick six month courtship, and Ben had never been happier.

Now he thought about Ann, wondering how her life had turned out. He hoped that her marriage had been as wonderful as his had been.

Ben returned from his reverie to hear the group trying to remember April's real first name.

"I think it was something like Maurine," Tom Aldrich was saying. "Whatever it was, with a last name like Showers, she was stuck with the nickname of April all through high school. That's the only name anyone remembers."

"Ann looks pretty good for a woman of our advanced years, don't you think?" Buddy remarked to Ben. "Never did figure out how you two avoided getting hitched. I hear her husband died a little over a year ago, about the same time as your Mary, I would guess."

Ann did look good, Ben thought. The years had been kind to her. She looked slim and athletic, and much younger than the other two with her.

With a smile to his colleagues, Ben got up and excused himself. "Time to check in on our prettier classmates," he said, and walked over to the ladies table.

April was the first to see him approaching and recognized him immediately.

"Ben Foxworth," she exclaimed. "Now you are a sight for sore eyes. And look at you—as trim and fit as a 20 year old." April, on the other hand, was showing the results of living on a very rich diet. Still had a pretty face, though.

Ben did take pride in his physical condition, working out at the gym every morning. And he felt good. But for some reason he found himself suddenly blushing.

"Hi, April. I see you're just as full of blarney now as you were in high school." Then he turned to Ann, who had arisen from her chair, and took her hands in his.

"Hello, Ann. How have you been?"

She is a good-looking woman he thought. Finely carved features, but with a few crow marks around her eyes that made her look even more beautiful and interesting. Her hair was tied back in a bun, with a few streaks of gray on each side of her head. It gave her a very elegant look.

"Hello, Ben," Ann replied. "You do look wonderful. It's good to see you."

They stood for a few minutes, studying each other, before April said, "Well, are you going to sit down and join us or not? And this here is Jean Wyatt—or Jean Smith as you would know her."

"Hi, Jean, good to see you again" Ben replied. For the life of him he couldn't place her. "Actually I came over here to invite you three gorgeous women to join us handsome men at the table in the back of the room," Ben pointed to where his classmates sat, who were now waving for them to come over.

So two tables were pulled together, the women joined the men, and the stories and jokes started all over again. Ann's married name was Hopkins, Ben discovered. Ann Hopkins. He didn't have a chance to talk with her on a personal level, but he did find out that she was staying with April, who had married a local boy, Henry Means, who was in a class ahead of Ben's. Together they ran a local flower shop. April and Henry were hosting the cocktail party for the class that evening at their home.

Finally the group broke up. Ben asked Ann if she would like to take a memory ride through the old town with him, but she declined, stating that she needed to help April get ready for the party.

Ben returned to his room, switched on CNN, and listened to the news. Still no leads into the bombing of the memorials in Washington D.C. last month—an amber alert for a 13 year old girl missing in Georgia——the senior senator from New Mexico retiring after 35 years in the Senate—an ACLU law suit against the county of Los Angeles to get them to remove the cross from their county emblem, which was one of several symbols depicting the history of the county. The cross was in memory of the missionaries who had moved up from Mexico and were the first to settle in the area.

They'll probably want the city to change its name from Los Angeles, too, Ben thought as he turned off the TV. *After all—the name "Those Angles" could be offensive to anyone not believing in them.*

Later in the morning Ben drove around town remembering old haunts—the home in which he had grown up, the high school, the athletic park, the cemetery where his parents were buried. He even parked his car on Main Street, and went into some of the old stores he remembered.

Finally he returned to the motel, haunted by memories—some from his high school days, and some from his years with Mary, and the happiness they had found.

CHAPTER THREE

Later in the afternoon Ben was awakened from a nap by the ringing of his telephone.

"Hey, Ben," it was Buddy Callahan. "Guess who I just ran into. Our old buddy, John Wilkerson! We're down here in the bar having a few beers. Come on down and join us. Just like old times." John Wilkerson was the other classmate with whom Ben had been really close. He had also been the best man at Ben's wedding. *Good old John.*

"Be right down, Buddy," Ben said. He splashed cold water on his face, combed his hair, and headed down to the bar.

It was truly like old times, just as Buddy had said. Within a very short time the awkwardness of being almost like strangers to each other had passed and it was as if they had never been apart. The Three Musketeers, they had called themselves in high school, and at this moment and at this place they slid easily into their old relationship.

Buddy had always been the more outgoing of the trio. Heavy set, blond curly hair—now with a grayish tinge—an amicable, broad face and ready smile that made you feel like you had known him your whole life. He was seldom serious; always ready for a prank, and the kind of guy at whom you could never get mad.

John on the other hand was the most reserved of the bunch. He had a slim build, dark hair and sharp features. He was also the smartest of the three. Straight "A" student, and President of their class.

Ben guessed he fell somewhere in between the two in temperament. Buddy always appealed to his happy-go-lucky side, while John was the one he turned to for more serious matters.

Each one of the trio brought the other two up to date on what had been happening in his life. Ben told them about Mary, and that he was living in a home all alone on 40 acres in the mountains above Colorado Springs. John hadn't known that Ben's wife had passed away.

"If ever there were two people made for each other, it was you two," he said.

John was a tax accountant, and had done well. He lived in Chicago and was happily married with three children. His wife, Beth, had not been able to come with him.

"She thought she would just be in the way, since she didn't know any of this gang," John stated. "And I'd probably just as soon she didn't meet you two anyway. Too many stories you could tell her. She thinks I'm a very upright citizen," he added with a laugh.

Both Ben and John produced the proverbial pictures of their children and grandchildren from their billfolds and passed them around.

"I have a wonderful daughter," Ben claimed, "who takes after her mother. She and her husband, and my two grandchildren, live in Seattle, so I don't get to see them as often as I would like. Since Mary passed on, Beth, my daughter, has really been bugging me to move nearer them. I think she believes me to be approaching old age and senility, and she needs to take care of me."

Buddy, they both knew, had become an agent for the FBI, never married, and according to him worked round the clock. "We're just like the postal workers—neither rain, sleet nor hail will deter us from our appointed rounds, protecting innocent citizens like yourselves from bad guys."

"Tell us about some of your exploits," John demanded. "A big FBI man like you must have a lot of exciting tales to talk about."

"Well," Buddy responded, a serious look on his face, "let me think. There was that time I got an award for saving a guy from Czechoslovakia. Seems that he had been invited by a lawyer to the lawyer's cabin in the mountains. They were out hiking one day when two bears jumped them. The lawyer got away, but one of the bears swallowed the Czech whole."

"Uh-oh," Ben moaned, sensing one of Buddy's tall tales coming on. And a lawyer story to boot.

"The lawyer called for help, and I got the case," Buddy continued. "When I got there the lawyer thought we still might be able to save the Czech if we could kill the bear that ate him. So he led me to where the bears were, one being a female and the other a male, and pointed to the male and shouted 'There! That's the one. The one on the left!"

"So I shot the female, the one on the right, and sure enough we were able to get the Czech out alive."

"OK, I'll bite," John said. "Why didn't you shoot the one on the left as the lawyer indicated?"

"Well, pretty obvious. Would you believe any lawyer that said the Czech was in the male?"

They all had a good laugh, and ordered another round of beers.

"Need to remember," Ben said, "we've got that cocktail party tonight for everyone over at April's. Can't party it up too much before then." They all agreed, and had another drink anyway.

A half hour later their voices had gotten a little louder, their laughter a little more boisterous, and their high school days didn't seem quite so distant. The ringing of a cell phone interrupted their revelry, and both John and Buddy automatically checked their waists where they carried their modern communication link to the outside world. Ben didn't carry a cell phone, so he watched with some amusement.

The call was on Buddy's cell. He mostly listened, grunted a few times, and hung up. He looked slightly annoyed, but quickly got back in the party mood of the group.

"Hey, remember the time we bombed Gene Sawyer's place with water balloons?" Buddy asked. This brought another round of laughter. Gene Sawyer had been somewhat of a nerd in high school. Always very serious about everything, and always very persnickety.

"I don't think I ever saw old Gene crack a smile," John said.

The escapade had happened one afternoon in the spring of their senior year. Graduation was only a week away, and they were all beginning to feel the constricting boundaries of school slipping away. They had been in study hall, and Buddy had thrown a paper wad at Gene, who was sitting at the next table.

Gene complained to the teacher, and as a result Buddy, John and Ben had to stay an extra hour in their seats after classes were over. The teacher automatically assumed that if any one of these three were guilty of some misdeed, they all had to be guilty. It was generally not a bad assumption.

When they got out of class, Buddy suggested they get some balloons, fill them with water, and go bomb Gene's house with them. This they proceeded to do—clumsily throwing the balloons onto the front porch like they were shooting free shots in a basketball game.

The only problem was that it wasn't Gene who came storming out of the house, but Gene's father. He chased the three for half a block before giving up. Gene had never seen the humor in the event, and had barely spoken to the three delinquents for the rest of the school year.

"You know, Gene still lives right here," Buddy said, having a little difficulty getting his words out coherently. "Went to college then on to law school, then came back here and opened a law firm. What say we have a toast to old Gene baby." Buddy raised his glass, and the other two joined him. Then after a moment, "Hey—I've got an idea. Since this is a reunion and all, what say we go pay old Gene a visit and bomb his house again. Just like we did 50 years ago. Seems like a reunion kind of thing to do."

Ben and John laughed loudly at the suggestion.

"Buddy—you've got to remember we're old men now. Need to be dignified and all that," John said, and once again raised his glass in the air.

"Dignified—that's us," Buddy replied. "You are right. We need to do this with great dignity and decorum." With that he rose unsteadily to his feet. "Come on. Let's go do it."

"Man, you're really serious about this, aren't you?" John asked.

"Well, isn't that what reunions are for? To relive the past?"

John stood and raised his glass. "Then let's do it," he said. "Here's to the Three Musketeers. We ride again."

Ben rose and the trio pressed their glasses together, and in unison, with slightly slurred voices, repeated their old slogan, "All for one and one for all."

So, with some misgivings on the part of Ben, the three left the bar, bought some balloons at the local drug store, filled them with water, and proceeded to the home of Gene Sawyer.

THE THIRD MUSKETEER

They were laughing softly to themselves as they started up the walk to Gene's house, awkwardly juggling the balloons.

"Shsss!" Buddy warned. "Don't want to make too much noise."

Just then the front door of Gene's house opened and two men came out. One was obviously a guest who was just leaving. The other was unmistakably Gene Sawyer. A little heavier, a little less hair, but the same perpetual scowl on his face. He sported a bushy mustache which was much darker than his hair, and a pair of thick, horn-rimmed glasses that made his eyes seem much larger than they really were.

The trio on the sidewalk stopped in mid-stride, suddenly feeling very sheepish, trying to hold on to balloons that wobbled and jiggled in their hands.

The gentleman leaving gave them an inquisitive look, and walked past them without speaking. Gene came to the edge of the porch and stared down at them.

"What do you want?" he asked without preamble.

There was a moment of embarrassed silence, then Buddy spoke up, "Hey Gene—it's your old classmates—Buddy Callahan, Ben Foxworth and John Wilkerson. Remember us? We were just having a beer or two remembering old times, and got to thinking about the time we—uh—came to visit you." With that he held up his balloon and gave a self-conscious laugh. "We thought it would only be neighborly to come say hello again, didn't we guys?" He turned to his companions, who by now were totally chagrined at what they had been about to do.

"Just wanted to say hello, and thought this would be kinda funny."

"I remember," Gene replied coldly. "As I recall, I didn't think it was particularly funny then, and God knows it doesn't seem funny now."

"Yeah, it was a bad idea," John replied. "Don't know what we were thinking. We really just wanted to drop by and say hello. You're looking good, Gene."

"Hey—you coming to the cocktail party over at April's this evening?" Buddy asked.

"Yeah, I'll be there," Gene replied. "Haven't missed a reunion yet. But sure haven't seen you three at any of them near as I can recall."

Another awkward silence followed.

"Well—as we said, just dropped by to say hello," Ben spoke for the first time. "Guess we'd better be getting back to the motel to get ready for this evening. See you there."

With that, the three scurried back to their car, still clutching the balloons in their hands. When they were settled in their seats John broke out in a loud chuckle, and soon all three were laughing hilariously.

"That's the dumbest thing I've done since the last time we tried this," John said between gasps.

"Did you see the look on Gene's face?" Buddy said. "I'd have recognized that scowl anywhere."

Ben hadn't laughed this hard for 20 years. "You guys are a bad influence on me," he said, trying to catch his breath. "I think I need to go back to Colorado."

"Well, I know I need to take a cold shower before tonight's party, and drink about a gallon of black coffee," Buddy replied.

Gene watched them drive off, a frown still etched deeply on his face.

CHAPTER FOUR

At the cocktail party the "Three Musketeers" were much more subdued than they had been that afternoon. The party was from 7:00 until 9:00 p.m., with appetizers and soft drinks furnished. If anyone wanted anything stronger it was a 'Bring Your Own Bottle" affair.

Ben mingled with the crowd, renewing old acquaintances, and remembering old times. Most of the classmates were in the back yard, standing in small groups or sitting at tables which were scattered around the lawn. Kon-tiki torches lit up the night sky, and gave a gala flavor to the evening.

Ann was busy assisting the hostess, and chatting with the guests. She had always been popular in high school, and was equally so this evening. A couple of times Ben found himself in the same group with Ann, but never had a chance to talk with her alone.

As Ben meandered around the yard, he noticed Buddy engaged in animated conversation with Gene Sawyer and a doughty, short woman who Ben supposed was Gene's wife. "Must be making amends for this afternoon," he thought, "and I probably should do the same."

"Hi Buddy—Gene," Ben said as he approached the trio. Gene shook his hand, introduced him to Elizabeth, his wife, and seemed much friendlier than he had appeared in the afternoon.

They chatted a while. Since both Ben and Gene were lawyers, much of the conversation centered around legal issues with a few lawyer jokes thrown in. Buddy soon excused himself, leaving the other two alone.

"I really need to apologize for this afternoon," Ben said. "Guess we had a couple beers too many, and thought it would be kinda like old times if we came to see you with the balloons. But after we got there it didn't seem such a good idea."

"No harm done," Gene replied amicably enough, although his wife gave Ben a dour look. "We did have some trying times back then, didn't we? Pretty funny now as we look back on it. So what aspect of the law do you specialize in? Criminal law?"

"No, no. Nothing so glamorous. Business law mostly. A few estates and wills. And you?"

"Pretty much the same. We don't get too much out of the ordinary in a small town, you know. How about Buddy? Does he still work for the FBI?"

"Yeah—old cloak and dagger Buddy," Ben smiled. "Says he's always working on a case. Even when he's on vacation."

"Well, I hope he's not working on one right here in Oldvil."

"I would doubt that. Not with our bunch of tried and true grads."

"If you ask me," Gene replied, "our tried and true grads, as you call them, are not much to be proud of. I don't know any of them that believe in anything other than themselves. Comes the day of reckoning I don't believe many in our class will be passing muster."

Oh,oh, Ben thought. *Sounds like old Gene has gotten religion.*

"Well," Ben replied, "I guess I don't know them that well. About their religious beliefs that is."

"As if they had any beliefs," Gene growled. "And that will be their downfall. People without faith in a power beyond themselves will not have the strength to stand up to adversity. Kill religion and you kill the nation."

Ben studied Gene a few minutes without replying. Gene seemed absorbed in his own thoughts, and hardly noticed when Ben said it had been good to see him again, and took his leave.

Ben tried once again to corner Ann, but without success. She did give him a warm smile, however, which Ben found himself returning.

Not long afterwards the guests began to leave. Ben told Buddy and John that he was going to stay and help clean up, so they went on back to the motel. Ben finally found himself sitting at a table alone with Ann.

"I hear the Three Musketeers had a little escapade going this afternoon," Ann said with a smile.

"Boy, word sure does get around," Ben said ruefully. "Where did you hear that?"

"Oh, Buddy told me. I think inside every grown man there must be a little boy just waiting to get out."

"The way I heard it," Ben answered, "is that inside every old man there is a young man wondering what the hell happened."

They chuckled at the thought, then in a more serious vein Ann asked, "And what about you, Ben? Is there a little boy inside you wondering what the hell happened?"

Ben took a while before answering. "Oh, I guess that little guy exists in everyone to some extent. You get so caught up in every day living—your job, your kids, being on the go—that you never think about how the days and weeks and months are slipping by. And then one day you wake up and your kids are gone, you retire from your job, and then—then one day you find your wife is gone, too." Ben paused before continuing. "Yeah, I guess to some degree you ask yourself 'What the hell happened.'"

Ann smiled, placed her hand on Ben's and gave it a small squeeze, and said, "But then there's that other voice that answers back, and says 'wasn't it wonderful?'"

"Yeah, I guess so. But how about you, Ann? Has life been kind with you?"

"Oh I would say so," Ann answered. "The usual ups and downs, I guess. Dave, my husband, and I were separated for almost a year, but then we got back together, and everything was wonderful the second time around. He quit his traveling sales job, we moved to Denver, and we started all over."

"Denver? I live just up from Colorado Springs. Here we are almost neighbors and didn't even know it."

"Colorado Springs? Well, we'll have to get together sometime and see a show or something."

"That would be great," Ben replied, wondering at the same time if he would ever really date another woman again.

They chatted for a while, talking about their children, their hobbies, and how they managed to keep busy as singles. When Ben checked his watch, he was surprised to see that it was almost 11:00. "It's getting late," he said, "Guess I'd better be getting back to my room." Ben hunted up April and Henry, thanked them for a great party, and headed out.

When Ben got back to the motel, he entered through the back security door, using his room key to gain admittance to the inner hallway. As he was about to unlock the door to his room, he noticed that Buddy's door, across the hall from his and up one room, was open. He hesitated a minute, then decided to see if Buddy would be interested in coming over to his room for a night cap.

He went to Buddy's door, knocked twice, and called out, "Hey Buddy—interested in a little hair of the dog before turning in?"

There was no answer, so Ben pushed the door open, and walked into the room. The lights were on and the TV was showing an old 1950's movie. He looked into the bathroom, which was empty, and walked further into the room. Then he saw Buddy on the floor on the other side of the bed. He was fully dressed, lying on his back with his eyes wide open, staring sightlessly at the ceiling. Blood covered his chest and made a pool on the floor. There was no sign of life in the inert body.

Ben stared at his friend with a growing sense of horror. He called out in a tremulous voice, although he knew there would be no answer, "Buddy?" And there was no answer.

Ben moved closer to where Buddy lay on the floor. He knelt beside the body and took Buddy's hand in his. It was still warm, but felt tepid to the touch. Shuddering slightly Ben felt for a pulse. There was none. Ben stared at the holes in Buddy's chest where the blood had seeped to the floor.

With a silent cry of dismay he rose, backed into the hallway, closed the door, and hurried back to his own room. With trembling hands he inserted his key card in the lock, rushed to the telephone, and called 911.

"There's been an accident at the Great Harvest Motel—I think a man has been shot. There's blood everywhere. Room 135. Send an ambulance and the police. Hurry!"

Ben answered the questions asked by the operator in a daze, hardly aware of his answers. Finally he hung up, and waited for the police to arrive.

His mind was in a flurry. Buddy dead—murdered almost certainly. But who would do such a thing? Ben thought of the good time the three of them had this afternoon, only a few hours earlier. Buddy had certainly given no hint that he might be in danger. Ben reached for the phone and rang John's room.

The phone rang several times before a sleepy voice answered.

"John—wake up," Ben said. "Something's happened to Buddy. I just found him in his room. The police are on their way. I think he's been murdered."

"What? Buddy? Dead?" John was instantly awake. "Where are you?"

"In my room. I've called 911. Get dressed and come on down. Hurry!"

"I'll be right there," John answered, and hung up.

The next few minutes seemed like an eternity to Ben. The thought of someone killing Buddy was overwhelming. Who could have done such a thing? All sorts of possibilities raced through Ben's mind; maybe someone from an old case Buddy had worked on; maybe a robber had forced his way into Buddy's room and shot Buddy when he had come back and surprised him; maybe it was just an accident.

John arrived at Ben's room just minutes before the police. Ben opened the door to let him in and saw the police and the night manager coming down the hall. Ben met them, told them he was the one that had found the body, and led them to Buddy's room.

The rest of the evening was a nightmare that Ben would forever remember. Buddy was definitely dead, shot multiple times in the chest. The police swarmed over the motel, and forensics people were hustling everywhere, taking pictures and checking for fingerprints. It seemed to Ben that half the police force must have been in and out of Buddy's room during the late night hours. Much, much later, Buddy's body was placed in a bag and taken to the mortuary.

"OK, Mr. Foxworth, let's go over your story one more time." The Chief of Police, Ervin Klaus, was a local man who had graduated three years behind Ben's class.

Ben took a deep breath. He realized that the police were just doing their job, but the whole process was wearing on his patience.

"As I said, I was returning to the motel from a class party—the same one that Buddy had been at earlier. I was about to enter my room when I noticed Buddy's door slightly open. I went down to talk with him and see if he might like a nightcap. I knocked at the door, there was no answer, so I walked in. I found him lying on the floor. I took his pulse, but there was no sign of life. I left the room, closing the door behind me, and called 911."

"And this John Wilkerson that was here with you when we arrived," Chief Klaus continued, "what would you say his relationship was to the deceased?"

"For God's sake," Ben exploded, "I have told you over and over. John and Buddy and myself were high school friends. We graduated 50 years ago. I saw John once at our 5th reunion—45 years ago. Buddy wasn't there. As far as I know neither John nor myself have seen or heard from Buddy for 50 years until today. I hardly think there would be any reason for John to suddenly up and kill him."

"Ok—ok. Just have to check out all the angles you know. No reason to get upset."

Much later John and Ben sat in Ben's room having a whiskey and water. Both were completely exhausted, too tired to go to bed, and still wanting to rehash the evening's events. It seemed so unreal.

"I'm not sure the Chief has all his marbles upstairs," John was saying. "He's questioning us like we were the prime suspects, and we haven't even seen Buddy in a lifetime."

"Just doing his job, I guess," Ben replied in a tired voice. "Maybe he's a little smarter than he appears. At least I hope he is."

They talked on for another hour, before John made his way back to his room. It was nearly 4:00 in the morning before Ben crawled into bed for a troubled and restless sleep.

CHAPTER FIVE

The next day dragged by slowly for Ben. He met John in the motel's cafeteria for a late breakfast. Once again they talked over the events of the previous evening. Buddy's death had put a damper on the entire reunion. Small groups of classmates, who had been so jovial the previous evening, sat around in the lobby or restaurant in subdued conversation.

"So are you going to the barbecue and football game this evening?" Ben asked.

"Yeah, I guess so," John replied. "Since I was class president our senior year, I kinda feel like I need to be there. I can tell you for sure, though, my heart isn't in it. How about you?"

"Don't know. I'll see how I feel when the time comes. It all seems kind of trivial somehow, now."

John nodded in understanding.

"I talked with my wife this morning," John said. "She was pretty upset over the whole thing. Wants me to come back home right away, but I told her I couldn't leave now."

While they were talking Chief Klaus walked in to the restaurant, scanned the room, spotted Ben and John, and walked briskly to their table. He looked like he hadn't had any sleep, although he had shaved and put on a newly pressed uniform.

"Good morning, Chief," Ben said. "You look tired. Any leads as to who might have killed Buddy?"

"Nothing. No finger prints. No obvious motive. Didn't take his billfold or money. I was hoping one of you might be able to give me some clue as to anything that might have been bothering him. Anything he said, or did out of the ordinary."

Ben and John gave each other a questioning look. "Can't think of anything," John finally replied. "Buddy didn't seem like a man worried about anything."

The Chief nodded, as though he had already known the answer. "One of the guests here at the motel—not one of your classmates—says he walked past Callahan's room around 10:30 last night and heard loud voices inside, like two men might have been arguing about something. Didn't see anything, though."

"What will happen to Buddy?" Ben asked. "As far as I know he didn't have any close family. No wife, no parents still alive, no brothers or sisters."

"We've contacted the FBI," the Chief responded. "They're flying someone here today to claim the body. Seems like he had made arrangements for just this kind of an eventuality with the Bureau. Maybe they all have to do that in their line of work for all I know." Then as he thought about it, added, "Probably not a bad idea at that. Maybe something I need to instigate in my force."

Later in the day Ben and John went over to April and Henry's house. Ann met them at the door.

"Oh Ben—and John," she said. "How awful about Buddy. I know how close the three of you were. I'm sure you must be in a state of shock."

She ushered them into the kitchen, where April was putting on coffee. Henry, her husband, was at work at their flower shop. They sat around the table and rehashed once again the terrible events of the previous night.

"It's funny," Ben said. "Here you are really close to someone all through your high school years, then you graduate and all go your separate ways. Fifty years later you get back together, and it's like nothing had happened in all that time. You're older, but just as close as when you left. And you wonder what all you might have missed by not staying in touch all of that time."

"Yeah," John agreed. "Makes you think that friendships are something special. Something you shouldn't take for granted, or leave behind."

They all sat for a moment, lost in their own thoughts. April broke the silence. "Didn't Buddy win some kind of trophy or something in basketball?"

"Most valuable player," John replied. "Led the team in both scoring and assists."

Ben chuckled. "Man, he was one tricky player. When he had the ball, his eyes, his shoulders, his whole body language would tell you he was about to do one thing, then he would do something else entirely."

"Misdirection," John added. "Misdirection was what he called it. Said you had to get people looking one way while you went the other."

"Guess it didn't work so well for him this time," Ben said, and once again they all lapsed into silence.

When Ben returned to the motel, he took a short nap to make up for the sleep he'd lost the night before. Later, as he showered and shaved, he decided he'd go to the cookout and ball game. After all, that's what he had come for, and Buddy would be the last one to have him moping around the motel.

As he was about to leave, there was a hard knock at his door. He opened it to find a woman and a black man facing him, both showing badges indicating they were with the FBI.

"Hi," the woman said. "My name's Suzie Becker and this here's Brady Jones. We're colleagues—and friends—of Buddy Callahan. Could we talk with you for a few minutes?"

The woman was short with a stocky, athletic build. She was not pretty in a classical sense, but her straw-colored hair, freckles, turned up nose and wide smile were appealing. Probably in her mid-forties, Ben guessed.

Jones was a slim man of indeterminate age, whose face at first glance seemed to have a stern, uncompromising look. Then you saw the twinkle lurking in the back of his eyes that changed his whole demeanor. He stepped forward and shook Ben's hand, saying, "I'm very pleased to make your acquaintance, Mr. Foxworth. And it's sorry I am about your friend. He was our friend also." Brady spoke with a strong Irish accent.

Susie saw the startled look on Ben's face, and with a broad smile said, "You have to get use to my partner. Although he's black, he thinks he's Irish."

"Sure and what else would I be?" Brady said to Suzie. "My mother was an Irish lass, and I myself was born and raised on the dear old island." Turning to Ben he continued, "My father was an American in the Air Force. He met my mother in London, they fell in love, and were married within a year. But three months after they were married, he was killed in an airplane accident. My mother returned to her family in Ireland, and six months later I made my way into the world. Never left the garden isle till I was 20 years old. As my old Irish grandfather used to say, if you're lucky enough to be Irish, you're lucky enough."

"You and your Irish grandfather," Suzie retorted. "I've certainly heard enough of him."

Ben laughed with them, and said, "Well, I guess I can say I've never met a black Irishman before. Mr. Jones, it is a pleasure."

As Ben held the door open for them, he saw John coming down the hall.

"This is John Wilkerson," Ben introduced John to the two FBI agents. "He and I and Buddy were very close in high school. Would you mind if he joins us?"

"Not at all," Suzie said. "Matter of fact we wanted to talk with John also, so now we can get you both at the same time."

"Buddy was a—special guy," she continued. "A personal friend. He sort of adopted me when I first came into the agency. He often talked of the both of you. I was always kind of envious of the great years he seemed to have had in high school. Mine weren't nearly so wonderful. Wrong side of the tracks, I guess."

Ben detected a note of bitterness in her voice.

"Your Chief Klaus called the FBI last night when they found Buddy's body," she continued. "Brady and I were asked to look into the—situation—and caught the red-eye special to Wichita this morning. We rented a car and got in here around noon. Been meeting with Klaus and his men and making funeral arrangements since we got here."

"Where will Buddy be buried?" Ben asked.

"Actually, right here," Suzie replied. "We've arranged for a small memorial service to be held Monday morning. We were hoping that the two of you might be able to stay over for it. Buddy would have liked it."

"No problem for me," Ben quickly replied.

"I think I can make it," John said. "Need to check with my wife and make sure it's OK with her. But she will understand."

"Do you have any idea who might have killed Buddy?" Ben inquired.

"Well, yes we do," Suzie replied. She gave Brady a quick look, and continued. "I guess it's OK if we level with you. But this is strictly between the four of us for now. It's actually a rather long story, but do you remember the bombings that occurred at the Washington memorials last month? We were able to identify a fingerprint found on one of the fragments of a briefcase that we think contained the bomb at the Korean Memorial. That, along with some other information that we have been able to obtain, has led us to believe that a Mr. Gene Sawyer may have been involved. Deeply involved."

Ben and John stared at Suzie in amazement.

"Gene Sawyer—you think Gene Sawyer blew up the Korean War Memorial?" John stammered.

Suzie let this information sink in before continuing. "We have reason to believe that there are three Americans—Anglos—who have become radical Islamic terrorists, and have formed a sleeper cell here in the states. I guess I shouldn't exactly call it a "sleeper" cell, because we believe that they were responsible for the bombings in Washington, and, what's worse, they are reportedly planning something even more deadly in the near future."

Ben's head was reeling—trying to grasp what the FBI agent was saying.

"The 'near future.' How soon is that?" he asked.

"Unfortunately it could mean any day now. Our intelligence was that it would be in the fall," Suzie said.

"And here it is September already," Brady said. "You can see it's very concerned we are. Time is running out on us. We had hoped to get more of a lead from your friend Sawyer before we arrested him, but it seems that is not to be."

"But the fact that you have him—isn't that likely to upset their time table?"

"No way of telling for sure," Suzie answered, "but I doubt that Sawyer was absolutely essential to their plan. In fact it might even serve to accelerate their action."

"We think Gene Sawyer was one of them," Brady said, "but we dinna have a thought who the other two might be. It's their Islamic names they go by—Fatim, Mullah and Al Khafi. Sawyer, we think, was Al Khafi. Buddy was here not just for your reunion, but to watch Sawyer for a few days to see if he could get any leads as to who the other two terrorists might be. We didn't want to arrest him just yet."

"But if you suspected Gene of being an international terrorist, wouldn't you have had more than one agent here checking on him?"

Suzie and Brady exchanged looks. "As a matter of fact, we did have another operative here working with Buddy. His body was found in a ditch this morning. Shot with the same gun that killed Buddy. A digital camera he had been carrying was missing."

Ben thought back to the telephone call Buddy had received the previous afternoon just before they had all gone to bomb Gene's house with the water balloons. Could there have been a connection? Had that call triggered Buddy's suggestion to go over to Gene's house?

"We think Sawyer somehow became aware that he was being watched and panicked," Brady continued. "We think he killed Joe, the other agent who had his house under surveillance, and then came over to the motel and shot Buddy."

"So have you arrested Gene?" Ben asked.

"Not yet," Suzie replied. "We had him in this afternoon and pretty much let him know that we had enough evidence to charge him, but then let him go, still hoping he might lead us to the other two members of his cell. We had his phone tapped several days ago, but so far he has been too careful to make any careless calls"

Ben and John were having a difficult time assimilating all of this.

"What we wanted to ask both of you was whether Buddy said anything to you that might give us a clue as to what he had found, or suspected, if anything."

Ben remembered once again their dismal visit to Gene's house with their water balloons. That had been Buddy's suggestion. "Buddy didn't say anything about suspecting Gene of anything," he said. "We only talked about Gene in relation to our high school days."

John nodded in agreement. They told the two agents about their aborted water balloon trip.

Brady and Suzie both sat up straight in their chairs when Ben mentioned the visitor he and John had seen leaving Gene's house when the three had arrived.

"Can you describe him?" Suzie asked.

Ben and John looked at each other, trying to remember what the man had looked like.

Ben spoke first, "You know, we really didn't pay too much attention. Here we were, caught trying to play some stupid high school prank and feeling very self-conscious, and there was Gene glaring down at us. I hardly noticed the visitor."

"He was thin, probably around 5-10," John joined in. "Dark complexion. I didn't look at his eyes. Tried to avoid them, as a matter of fact."

"Would you say that he was Mid-eastern then?" Brady asked.

"Guess he could have been," John replied. Ben nodded in agreement.

"Well, we're really looking for an Anglo," Suzie observed. "Or at least we think we are. Still, it might be useful. Think you could identify him if you saw him again?"

Both John and Ben paused a minute before replying. "I guess we could give it a try," John said.

"Good. We can have some photos sent to us—kind of our rogue's gallery—could be here by tomorrow."

"Buddy received a telephone call just before he came up with the idea of going to Gene's house," Ben said. "Could that have been from his cohort, the other agent—what was his name—Joe? Could he have been calling Buddy to say that Gene had a visitor, and that is why Buddy talked us all into going over to Gene's house? To see who the visitor might have been?"

"Sure and I think that is probably the way it happened," Brady replied.

"What I don't understand," Ben continued, "is how someone like Gene Sawyer could become an Islamic terrorist. Do you think they are taking orders from Al Quaida?"

"Don't think so," Brady said. "We know our home grown terrorists have been trying to contact Al Quaida, but don't believe they've been successful so far. They seem to be acting strictly on their own."

That's probably the source of their intelligence, Ben thought. *Intercepted phone calls or messages on the Internet.*

"We never even heard of Islam when we were growing up here in Oldvil," Ben said. "How could someone like Gene be exposed to a religion so foreign to us and become so embittered with his own people that he thought it was all right to kill them?"

"It's really not that difficult," Suzie said. "People get disaffected with our society and look for something else to believe in. Usually it starts with the government. You know—how the government is corrupt and in league with international corporations for money and power. They get to thinking that the government is taking away all of our liberties and spying on everyone, and can't be trusted."

"These people consider themselves to be morally in the right," Brady added. "They look at our society and see greed in the corporations, and in our politicians. And complete self indulgence among the American people. Divorce, which used to be a rarity, now a common occurrence. Homosexuality becoming an accepted form of behavior. Modern rap music encouraging violence against law enforcement officers. Drugs everywhere."

"They get to thinking that our nation has become totally decadent, and something radical needs to happen to change things," Suzie said.

"Well—that doesn't sound too bad," Ben observed. "Where is it we go to sign up?"

"The difference, my lad," Brady continued, "is when you cross the line from thinking of people as human beings and start seeing them as pawns in a giant chess game, to be sacrificed for a greater good. Then it doesn't bother you that some, or many, have to die to achieve a better world."

"For these people," Brady said, "Islam offers a viable option to the corruption we see in the Western World. A religion that demands total obedience every hour of the day to a strict set of moral values. Many Christians, I've noticed, only practice their religion on Sundays, and even then only if it is convenient. Islam on the other hand requires worship of God three times a day, so the teachings of Islam are never far from their thoughts. The problem, as it has been with every religion through the ages, is when extremists distort the religion to justify violence on those who disagree with them."

"But where would Gene have come in contact with Islamists?" John asked.

"As you suggested," Brady replied, "it probably wasn't here in Oldvil. But there is an Islamic mosque near Bamford Law School in New York City where Sawyer got his law degree. We think he may have been exposed to and become a follower of Islam back there. We've checked the mosque out, and there is no evidence of any kind of link between them and any terrorist organization, but still, one or more worshipers could have been secretly recruiting members for Al Qaeda."

"That is our one hope of finding who the other two members of the cell might be," Suzie joined in. "They may have gone to the same law school and been recruited in the same way as Sawyer. The Department is checking out all of Sawyer's classmates even as we speak."

"But how did you get all this information about the three Anglos and their Islamic names?" John asked.

"I'm afraid that comes under the heading of classified information. But we do have our sources."

"Well, I understand you have a football game to go to," Suzie said. "We won't keep you any longer. But tomorrow we should have the photos we would like you to look at. Also, I am going to get an artist flown in from our office to draw a sketch of the man you saw at Sawyer's, based on your description. In the meantime if you think of anything that might be important, let us know. Here is my card with my cell phone number—call me anytime." She handed both John and Ben a business card. Brady also extended his card to each.

The two FBI agents left, leaving Ben and John in complete turmoil, still too shocked to think clearly. At length John said, "I guess if we're going to the barbecue and game, we'd better get moving."

"Yeah," Ben answered. But his heart wasn't in it.

CHAPTER SIX

Ben couldn't keep his attention on the game. His mind kept playing and replaying visions of Buddy lying on the floor of the motel room, and of the conversation with the two FBI agents. Off to the west giant flashes of lightning began to light up the sky, revealing huge dark clouds headed their way. Each display brought the storm closer, and finally, with 2 minutes to go and Oldvil ahead 24-7, the rain started to fall. As the crowds rushed to their cars Ann yelled for Ben and John to come over to the Means home for desert.

As they sat around the kitchen, trying to dry out and enjoying home made ice cream and coffee, Ann asked Ben, "When are you headed back to Colorado?"

"I was planning on going back Sunday, but now I'm staying for Buddy's memorial service on Monday. Guess I'll leave Monday night, or Tuesday sometime. How about you?"

"Same with me. I feel I really need to stay for the funeral. I'm in no special rush to get back, as long as I don't over-stay my visit here."

Henry Means quickly assured Ann that she was more than welcome to stay as long as she liked. Henry was a big man, and like April, showed the effects of over indulgence at the dinner table. His mid section extended well ahead of the rest of his body. Ben remembered him vaguely from high school days.

Henry had been somewhat of a maverick as he recalled. Always questioning authority and several times being on the edge of expulsion from school.

"So Henry," Ben said, "how did you and April happen to get into the nursery business?"

"Just something we enjoy doing, I guess. You may remember that after high school I went to Kansas State. Got my degree in agriculture. After I graduated I spent several years in Egypt working with a church group trying to teach improved farming methods to the locals. It was something I enjoyed, and when I came back to the States and met April we decided that it would be fun to run a nursery. I kinda like being my own boss. With April there to help run the place I can pretty much come and go as I like."

"Sounds like you chose well," Ben said. Then turning to Ann asked "Anything exciting going on in your life these days?"

"In a couple of weeks," Ann said, "a group of us are going to Albuquerque for the international balloon festival. I'm really looking forward to that."

"That really is a great show," Ben agreed. "It's one of the most colorful sights I have ever seen."

"Do you sit in the stands to watch them take off," April asked.

"No—much better," Ben replied. "You actually walk around the field where the balloons are being inflated and launching. It really brings it up close. They usually have around six or seven hundred balloons going up in waves. If the winds are just right they can all hover over the field. What they call the box affect. The winds blow south at one elevation and north at a higher one. So if a balloon ascends and descends to catch these winds it moves in a box-like pattern. When the sky is filled with six hundred balloons of all sizes, shapes and color it actually takes your breath away."

"Sounds wonderful," April said.

John, checking his watch, announced that he was headed back to the motel to call his wife. It was late, but she would still be up, worrying about him. "Drop in for a nightcap when you get back to the motel, if it isn't too late," he told Ben.

Shortly after he left, April and Henry turned in for the night, leaving Ben and Ann sharing a last cup of coffee.

"Who is the group you're going to Albuquerque with?" Ben asked.

"Oh just some people from a country club we—I—belong to. Three women and two men."

"Seems like an uneven number. Are you the odd man—or should I say woman—out?"

Ann hesitated before answering. "Well, probably not. One of the men—Donald Klein—is a special friend. We have been seeing quite a bit of each other since Dave—my husband—passed away. He has been very helpful and kind to me."

Ben couldn't help feeling a little pang of jealously.

"Well, I guess I shouldn't be surprised. You are too attractive and too full of life to be sitting around by yourself all day."

Ben thought about his own daily routine. He loved his home in the mountains, and never wanted to give it up for city life. But he had to admit that since Mary's death it had become somewhat lonely. Especially in the evening, when he stoked up a fire in the family room and put on some of the old tapes. Nat King Cole and Coleman Hawkins and others from the romantic era. Mary seemed very close at these times, and he found himself talking with her, telling her about the day's activities. *Dear God, will I ever get over missing her?*

After a moment's silence, with each lost in his and her own thoughts, Ben said, "Did I tell you that Mary came to see me after her death?"

Ann looked at him in surprise. "What do you mean—came to see you?"

"Just that. Several days after the funeral I woke up early one morning and there she was—sitting in a chair by the bed, smiling at me. It was a loving smile, the kind she would get when our child had done something special to make her proud, or some other occasion when she was perfectly happy and pleased with life."

"Are you serious? Was it a dream?"

"I guess that would have to be the official explanation," Ben replied. "But I know it wasn't a dream—it was real. Very real."

"Did she say anything?" Ann asked.

"She said that she loved me, and that I should be careful at the reunion. Then she was gone."

"How strange," Ann said.

"Yeah. The part that I really have to wonder at is when she told me to be careful at the reunion. I thought, 'What reunion?' I hadn't been to any kind of a reunion for 40 years—high school or college, and I certainly didn't have any plans to attend one now. Then, two days later, out of the blue, I got the letter about our high school 50th reunion. Was that prophetic or not? It seemed to me that based on what Mary had said, it was preordained that I would go. So I did, and here I am."

"But what about telling you to be careful?"

"I've thought about that. Curiosity alone about having to be careful at the reunion would have been enough to bring me back. And now all this stuff with Buddy and Sawyer—makes a body wonder. I haven't told another soul about seeing Mary, even my daughter Beth. She'd probably want to commit me to the old folk's home. But I know it wasn't a dream. I saw her—she was there, and she spoke to me."

"You know," Ann said, "I had somewhat of a similar experience when my father died. Or I should say Vickie, our daughter, did. Dad had been in intensive care in the hospital for a week before he gave up the ghost, so to speak. The next morning after he passed away, we were at the breakfast table and Vickie, who was four years old at the time, matter of factly stated that Grandpa had been in her room last night. Dave and I just stared at her. We hadn't figured out yet just how to break the news to her that he had died. Finally Dave asked her if Grandpa had said anything. She said, no, he was just smiling at her at the foot of the bed while she slept. We never did come up with an explanation for that one."

"We never do," Ben said. "When things like that happen that are outside of our range of comprehension, we just say it must have been a dream, or trick of the imagination, or strange coincidence, and put it out of our mind. But I've heard too many stories like this to try to pass them off with what we think is a rational explanation. I firmly believe there are things in this life that we just don't have an answer for."

"You miss her a lot, don't you?" Ann asked.

Ben didn't answer immediately, staring hard at his cup of coffee. Finally he said, "Yeah, I do. And it makes me so angry I can hardly stand it. It just isn't fair that she should have been taken from me when we both had so much to look forward to."

Ann nodded. "I know what you mean. I was angry when David died. But I could never quite decide who I should be angry with."

"I didn't have any trouble on that score," Ben replied with a bitterness edging into his voice. "At first I was angry with Mary for leaving me. If she really loved me how could she have done that, I thought. Then I shifted my anger to the doctors. Did they really know what they were doing? Was their treatment appropriate? Then it was God's turn. He could have prevented it if He really wanted. Finally I realized I was the one I was really mad at. Had I done everything I could to protect her? Had I loved her enough to have prevented this?"

"Ben, you can't blame yourself for what happened. It certainly wasn't your fault. Or anyone else. Things like this just happen. You need to be thankful for the wonderful life you had, not mad because it ended."

"I know. That's what I keep telling myself."

Ben finished his coffee, looked at his watch, and announced it was time for him to leave. Ann saw him to the front porch. The moonlight shone on her face as she stood by the stairs, highlighting her soft features and deep blue eyes. Ben studied her in silence for a moment before turning and heading down the walk. He heard the door close softly behind him.

As Ben turned to his car he noticed that the rain had stopped, but thick clouds still hid the moon and stars from view. The streets were filled with puddles in the low spots, and the grass glistened brightly whenever his headlights swept over the yards.

When he got back to the motel he went to John's room, and knocked on the door. Getting no response, he rapped a little louder. Still no answer from within. A sudden chill shot through his body, going all the way from the back of his neck down to his toes. He tried the door, but it was locked.

The vivid memory of finding Buddy's body the previous night swept over him, and he found himself trembling as he stood before John's door. *Dear God—please not again.* Ben looked up and down the hallway, and thought about pounding on the door more loudly, but decided to go to his own room to try calling John on the phone. If John were sleeping the telephone would surely awaken him.

He unlocked the door to his room and started to push it open, but stopped half way. He remembered Mary's warning to be careful at the reunion. A premonition of danger, or a wave of fear, he couldn't tell which, held him in his tracks. He stood for a moment with the door partially open, then abruptly pulled it closed without entering. At the same instant the wood splintered at his head as a bullet slammed through the door from inside his room, narrowly missing his temple and burying itself in the wall behind him. Only then was he aware of the sound of a gun being fired.

Ben turned and was about to run towards the front of the motel, to the office, but realized it was too far down a long, well lighted hall. Instead he sprinted to the back door from which he had just entered. As he slammed the glass door open he looked back over his shoulder and saw a figure dressed in black with a hood over his head standing just in front of Ben's room. He was clutching a pistol with both hands, which was aimed directly at Ben.

Ben pushed through the outside door when something hard slammed into his shoulder, almost knocking him over with its force. Again, belatedly, he was aware of the sharp crack of a pistol.

Ben rushed into the night air searching for help or a place to hide. There was no sign of anybody else in the parking lot. Again he looked longingly at the motel office, but it was too far away. He ran between two parked cars and across the lot into a thick field of bushes and trees. He lunged straight ahead for ten paces then turned sharply to his right. After a few more steps he turned to his left and ran deeper into the woods. The ground was soft from the rain which had fallen earlier and the damp leaves softened the sound of his footsteps.

Ben found himself gasping for breath as he staggered through the dense undergrowth, and then became aware of a stabbing pain in his shoulder. Looking down he saw a bright stream of blood running down his shirt.

The burst of adrenaline he had experienced earlier was now seeping away, and Ben realized he could go no further. Looking around he spotted a fallen tree just to his left, and fighting off a deep sense of exhaustion, he crawled over the trunk of the tree and slumped down behind it.

He strained to hear some sound of his pursuer, but for a few minuets there was nothing except the sharp rasp of his own breathing, which he tried desperately to control. The seconds ticked by and still there was no sound. Just when he began to think his attacker might have turned back, the soft thud of footsteps broke the night silence.

Ben hugged the ground and made himself as small as possible. The gentle squishing of shoes stepping on wet leaves came closer. A twig snapped on a branch of the fallen tree under which Ben was hiding. Then the woods became deathly quiet once again, and Ben realized that the man was standing just on the other side of the fallen tree.

He felt around for something he could use as a weapon, and found a small rock half buried in the damp soil. He grasped the rock, and tensed his body, ready to leap up and attack his assailant. He prayed he had enough strength left to do this swiftly, but everything now seemed to be happening in extreme slow motion.

Then he heard the distant sound of sirens. *The police were coming!*

For several moments longer there was no sound other than that of the approaching police cars, and then Ben heard the soft tread of footsteps headed back to the motel.

Ben lay on the ground without moving. He realized he was drifting in and out of consciousness. With a supreme effort he pulled himself to his feet and staggered back towards the motel. Now he could see the flashing lights of several vehicles in the parking lot.

Come on, Ben, he told himself, *don't stop now. Keep going. If you fall they could be weeks in finding you.*

With a great effort he pushed through the last shrubs and into the open. He stumbled half way across the pavement towards the police cars before he fell to his knees. Through a haze he heard someone shouting. He tried to make out the words, but they were indistinguishable. Then darkness enveloped him.

CHAPTER SEVEN

Once again Ben was aware of voices. Only this time they weren't shouting, but were softly modulated and melodious in tone. *Women's voices*, he decided. He strained to understand what they were saying, but they didn't seem coherent. The words drifted in and out of his mind without making sense.

After a while the voices seemed to become stronger, and he was able to make out some of the words. *Where am I?* Ben thought. Then vivid memories began to form in his mind. The door to his room erupting in splinters just a few inches from his head from a bullet fired from within. Knocking on John's door with no answer. Struggling through the woods with someone after him.

The cobwebs in Ben's mind evaporated and he became fully alert. He turned his head, and saw Ann sitting beside him, talking to someone at the foot of the bed. It was the FBI agent, Suzie.

"John," he croaked. Clearing his throat he repeated in a stronger voice, "John Wilkerson. Is he alright?"

"Oh, Ben. You're awake," Ann exclaimed in obvious relief. "We've been so worried about you. You lost so much blood. But the doctor says you're going to be all right." Suzie arose from her chair at the foot of the bed and stood behind Ann.

"Is John OK?" Ben repeated, searching the faces of the two women for an answer.

They exchanged glances, before Suzie said, "I'm afraid your friend, John, is gone. He was shot in the head last night. Undoubtedly by the same person that tried to kill you. Did you get a look at him? Are you able to tell us what happened?"

Ann gave Suzie a disapproving look. "Suzie, for crying out loud—he just woke up."

The nurse came hustling in, obviously aware from her nursing station that Ben had regained consciousness. "Ah, I see you are back with us Mr. Foxworth. If you ladies will excuse us I need to take his vitals." Ann and Suzie moved to the other side of the bed. Ben hardly noticed the nurse as she took his temperature and blood pressure. A slow anger was seeping through his whole being. Buddy dead, and now John.

He turned to Ann, "You know, I came to see my old friends, not to bury them. If Gene Sawyer did this I hope his soul rots in hell." The nurse frowned at this remark, told him to get some rest, and left the room.

"I'm afraid we have some more bad news," Suzie told him. "We got a call from Sawyer's wife late last night. She had taken a Tylenol PM and turned in. But she woke up later to discover that Sawyer hadn't been to bed. She got up to see if anything was wrong and found him in the den, shot through the head."

"But how could that be?" Ben asked. "Didn't you have him under surveillance?"

"We did," Suzie said. "Your local police chief had assigned one of his men to keep a watch on the house. But someone must have snuck in from the back. Our man says he didn't hear a thing, but I guess a pistol doesn't make that much noise, especially if the TV is turned up."

Ben thought back to the previous evening when someone had shot at him at the motel. Contrary to what Suzie had just said, it seemed to him that a gun made quite a bit of a racket. *A down right explosion*, he thought.

"Suzie, what's going on here?" Ben demanded. "Two of my friends have been murdered, one of my classmates is a terrorist, I've been shot at, and now the prime suspect is dead. Will you tell me what in the hell is happening?"

"We're still trying to sort it all out. We're pretty sure that the man you saw leaving Sawyer's house was one of the terrorists. Fatim or Mullah. Do you think he might have been the man who chased you last night?"

Ben thought for a moment, remembering once again the figure of the assassin standing in the hallway aiming a gun at him as he crashed through the doors into the night.

"You've got to realize I only had a fleeting look at him, and running for my life. I don't know that I could testify on this in court, but my impression is that it was someone else. This guy seemed shorter and maybe a little stockier than our mystery man."

Suzie nodded. "That would tie in with our latest theory," she said. "We're still waiting for the final word from ballistics, but it appears that the gun used to kill Sawyer is the same one used on Buddy and our other agent. Which lets Sawyer out as the prime suspect in those attacks. The bullets fired at you, though, and which killed John, came from a different gun. Here's what we think—our current working hypothesis."

"We believe our three terrorists were getting together here in Oldvil to finalize their plans for their next attack, not knowing that Sawyer had just been put under FBI surveillance. Our mystery man called on Sawyer and then discovered to his dismay that he could now be identified by Buddy and our other agent. It was imperative that he retrieve any photos or other evidence they might have, and to put them out of operation."

"The next day he probably met with the third member of their team—Fatim or Mullah—whichever is which—and they decided that Sawyer had to go. He was no longer useful to them, and in fact could blow their operation completely. Also they decided that you and John had to be dealt with because you two could also identify the mystery man if you ever saw him again. So our mystery man took care of Sawyer last night while terrorist number three waited at the motel for you and John. This scenario would seem to fit the facts as we know them at this time."

Ben thought for a minute. "You said you would have some pictures for me to look at today. Do you have them?"

"I do." Suzie replied. "Are you sure you're up to that right now?" Ben nodded, and sat upright in his bed.

Much later Ben had reviewed all of the photos that Suzie showed him, but none of them looked like the visitor he had seen at Gene's house. The police artist arrived, as Suzie had promised, and drew a sketch of the man to the best of Ben's ability to describe him.

"You said the man could have been a mid-easterner," Suzie stated. "According to our information, all three of the terrorists were Anglos. Of course, I guess 'Anglo' could mean almost anything other than African-American or Oriental."

"Who were the people in the photos you had me look at?" Ben asked.

"Kind of a hodge—podge. People with known or suspected terrorist connections. And all of Mr. Sawyer's graduating class from the Bamford Law School. Just a few long shots. I didn't hold out much hope that we would find our man from the pictures, but we have to try. Sometimes we get lucky."

"The pictures from Sawyer's graduating class. Were they strictly from his class, or did they include those from classes preceding him and following him?"

"Just those from his class. Possibilities get too numerous if you branch out too far."

"What about John? Have arrangements been made for his body?"

"The remains are being shipped to a mortuary in Chicago today. His wife is planning a memorial at his church at the end of the week."

The door swung open and Brady Jones walked in.

"Greetings and God be with you old friend," he said to Ben. "Glad to see you're back among the living. You're a pretty valuable man, you know. It's myself that's been assigned to look after you."

Ben gave him a questioning look. "Assigned to me?"

"Sure, to keep the bad guys away."

Suzie interjected. "You are our only link to this mystery man. One attempt has already been made on your life. From now on Brady here will be sticking to you like a fly to a honey pot. We don't want to lose you after all of this."

"So its friends we're to be," Brady said. "As my dear old Irish grandfather used to say, may the hinges of our friendship never grow rusty."

Ben groaned, then asked, "And for how long do I get to enjoy your company?"

A frown came across Brady's face. "Probably not long," he replied. "If our intelligence is correct, they mean to move any day now on their next attack. I dinna think time is on our side."

Just then a call came through on Ben's cell phone, which was lying by his bed. Ben picked it up. It was his daughter on the line.

"Dad—are you all right?" she asked in a worried voice. "A nurse called last night and left a message that you were in the hospital but that you were OK. We were out and didn't check for messages when we got home. What's going on? Are you sick or what?"

"I'm OK. Seems there was a shooting at the motel and I happened to be in the wrong place at the wrong time. Have a slight wound in the shoulder is all. I didn't know anyone had called you. I guess they must have gotten your name from my billfold. You'll be pleased to know I have a card in there identifying you as next of kin if anything should happen to me."

Ben definitely wasn't going to worry Beth with the events of the past few days.

"This is just exactly what I've been trying to tell you, Dad. This is what I am afraid of. Here you are in the hospital with no one to look after you. You need to move here so I can take care of you when things like this happen. With the kids involved in almost everything there is to be involved with, it's impossible for me to just up and leave to fly back to Colorado."

Ben reminded her that he wasn't in Colorado anyway, but that didn't deter her argument any. She was convinced that Ben needed to sell his home and move closer to them.

"You see the grandkids so seldom they hardly remember you from one visit to another."

Ben tried to assure her that he was still of sound mind and almost sound body, and that everything was OK. But he had to admit that moving closer to Beth and her family had a certain appeal. Sometime he might have to give the idea some consideration, but not for now.

* * * * *

THE THIRD MUSKETEER

The next morning Ben was feeling much better, and was up and around and grouching about how soon he could get discharged. Ann and April came to see him about mid-morning. Ben and the ladies chatted intermittently while watching CNN on the TV in the room. It seemed to Ben that not much had happened in the outside world. The missing girl in Georgia had been found unharmed with her high school boy friend—the New Mexico Attorney General, Anthony Sanchez, had thrown his hat in the ring for the Senate seat being vacated by Claude Hermosa, the retiring lawmaker—there were new bombings in Baghdad with no casualties—and the ACLU was now suing the state of California to prohibit all employees from wearing any religious symbol, such as crosses, during their working hours.

Ann was beside herself. "I just don't understand any of this," she said. "Now a person can't even wear a necklace with a cross on it? How could we have gotten so far from sanity? Something millions of people have no problem with has to stop because some atheist might be offended? God save us all!"

Ben chuckled. "Well, the atheists, or more correctly the lawyers with the ACLU, are calling the shots these days. Along with a very liberal set of judges who interpret the laws to their own liking rather than as to the intent of the legislation. And I guess if you are a state employee, representing the government to the public, and you display a religious symbol, that somehow means the state is endorsing it"

"You mean to tell me that I'm infringing on someone's constitutional rights if I wear a cross around my neck?" Ann said. "Come on, Ben. That's so ridiculous that it isn't even funny."

"What about this whole separation of church and state thing, Ben?" April asked. "You're a lawyer. How is it we went for 200 years with no problem and now all of a sudden we have to deny our entire heritage because it might hurt someone's feelings?"

"Actually, the Constitution doesn't say anything about separation of church and state," Ben observed. "That is some judge's interpretation. The only thing the Constitution says is in the First Amendment, where it states, and I think I am quoting it correctly, 'Congress shall make no law respecting an establishment of religion, or prohibiting the free exercise thereof.'"

"That's it?" Ann said. "That's all it says?"

"That's it," Ben replied. "They refer to it as the 'entitlement' clause, and that's been the basis for all the subsequent judgments on government and religion. Actually, it is pretty obvious what the framers had in mind. Many of them came from a country that had established a national church such as the Catholic Church, or the Church of England. In fact, just about the time that our constitution was being written a young man in Scotland was executed for heresy against the church. They didn't want that to happen here—Congress passing a law making church doctrine a law of the land—so we have the first amendment. There is nothing that says that Government can't or shouldn't recognize religion, or acknowledge a higher power. Our ancestors just didn't want Government passing any laws about it, or designating one church as the official church of the nation."

"Well, that's a far cry from where we are today," April said. "What I don't understand, if the amendment only referred to Congress passing laws, why does that keep our local community from having a nativity scene in the park at Christmas?"

"For most of our nation's history the courts held that laws effecting Congress did not extend to states," Ben replied, "but that all began to change in 1947 in a Supreme Court decision involving a fellow named Emerson. He sued the Board of Education in a New Jersey town because the state was reimbursing schools, including parochial schools, for the cost of transporting students. That was, in legalize, a seminal case that started the court down an activist road that brought us to where we are today."

"And now you can thank the American Civil Liberties Union—the ACLU—for rigorously following up on that," Ben continued. "What started out as a great organization, one dedicated to making sure citizen's civil rights weren't violated, has become a terrorist organization of its own."

"Terrorist organization?" Ann asked. "What do you mean?"

"The ACLU has become an activist political agency pushing its own agenda. They don't just come to the defense of someone who might claim his or her rights have been violated, they go out aggressively looking for and encouraging people to file law suits so that they can establish their own distorted view of the world. They have amassed immense wealth, so they can threaten a city or county with a massive law suit if they don't bend to the ACLU's desires. Like suing the county of Los Angeles because they have a cross on their county emblem depicting the missionaries who settled the area. Most cities or counties are unable to afford this kind of litigation, so they bow to the threats of the ACLU, and remove the cross, or whatever it is that the ACLU wants removed"

"But it's a stretch of the imagination to call them a terrorist group, isn't it?" Ann asked.

"Well, I guess I get carried away on the subject," Ben said. "But when a big bully comes in and threatens you with a huge law suit if you don't do what they want, even though what they want is against the desires and aspirations of the majority of people, I'd say that borders on terrorism."

"So laws are debated in Congress by lawmakers and ratified by the people, and then a judge, who has never been elected to anything, or the ACLU, come in and subvert the intent of the law to their own ends?"

"That's about the size of it. At least, that's my own parochial view of things. You should probably talk with someone on the other side of the issue to get their view. I'm sure the people at the ACLU firmly believe in what they are doing, and that is to make sure there is never any acknowledgement of God or a higher power in any branch of our national or local government. They are protecting the sensitivity of the atheists."

"Actually," Ann pondered," when you dictate the absence of religion in Government to protect atheists, aren't you in affect creating an atheist government? One that does not recognize God? And atheism is a religion of its own, isn't it? A religion that believes there is no God. So if you have on the one hand Christians who believe in God and on the other atheists who do not believe in God, why should the atheist's rights be given preference over Christians? Seems to me that this is violating the constitution, that you are making a law outlawing religion. And what was the other part of that amendment—Congress is not to pass any laws prohibiting the free exercise of religion? What do you call it when the Government outlaws any observance of religion within their jurisprudence?"

"I agree," Ben remarked. "Judges should have stuck with the original amendment, and simply said that Congress could not pass any laws regarding religion, which was what the writers of the Constitution intended. Now they are making laws saying we cannot have any expression of religious thought within the halls of Congress. Or within city hall, or the public library, or the Post Office, or even a government contractor. And I agree, seems like that is making laws restricting the free exercise of religion—just what the Constitution didn't want."

Later that night Ben thought about this conversation. He had surprised himself when he referred to the ACLU as a terrorist organization, but the more he considered it the more apropos it seemed. Then he thought about something Gene Sawyer had said at the cocktail party before Buddy was killed. "People who don't have faith in a power beyond themselves won't be able to stand up to adversity. Kill religion and you kill the nation."

These thoughts troubled Ben as he drifted off to a restless and shallow sleep.

CHAPTER EIGHT

Jackie was a pleasing plump, natural blond, with a businesslike and somewhat grumpy disposition. Nevertheless she was Ben's favorite nurse. He waited till she came on duty at 8:00 Monday morning before announcing that he was going to check out of the hospital long enough to attend Buddy's memorial service at the First Presbyterian Church at 11:00.

Jackie pursed her lips, looked thoughtful, and said, "I don't recall your doctor saying anything about that. Just where did you come by this piece of information?"

"The information didn't come *to* me, Jackie. It came *from* me. Buddy was a special friend, and I feel well enough to go. It won't hurt me to be out of your tender loving care for a couple of hours, although I admit I will miss your sunny disposition."

Jackie gave him a dour look, but couldn't keep the smallest trace of a smile away from the corners of her mouth. She might be Ben's favorite nurse, but in return he was currently her favorite patient, although she would never admit to it.

Brady, sitting in a chair in the corner of the room, seemed to enjoy the spirited exchange.

"You may have heard that old expression, Mr. Foxworth," she replied, "that the doctor knows best. I readily admit that you have received the best possible care under our auspices, but you must remember that you lost an awful lot of blood, and that bullet really tore up your shoulder. I don't want you to screw up all of the magnificent and hard work we've done on you by doing something foolish."

"At least let me get cleaned up," Ben said. "Can you disconnect me from this IV contraption so that I can shower and shave?"

Jackie muttered something under her breath, but pulled the plug from the needle stuck in Ben's arm. "I'll leave the needle in place," she said, "so that it will be easier to hook you back up when you're finished."

At that moment Ann walked into the room carrying Ben's suit, shirt, tie, belt, socks and shoes.

"Good morning everyone," Ann said. "Ben, I got your clothes from the motel just like you said."

Jackie rolled her eyes, shook her head, and left, muttering that she would talk with the doctor when he came in.

"What's the matter with her?" Ann said.

"Oh, just her usual sunny disposition. She seems to think I shouldn't be going to the memorial. But she'll come around."

"Ben, are you sure you are up to this? She may be right."

"Don't you start in on me too. I wouldn't go if I didn't feel all right. Honestly."

"OK. If you say so. I'll be by a little after nine to pick you up. See you then."

The doctor dropped in an hour later, and said it was fine with him if Ben wanted to go to the service. "Just remember, don't over do, and if you get dizzy sit down and rest till you feel better."

When Ann came back she had a tall, rather stout individual, with a mustache and neatly trimmed Van Dyke beard, trailing behind her. He had a thick head of black hair, although there was a grey dusting showing in the beard. All in all a very large and very distinguished looking gentleman.

"Ben, I would like you to meet a very good friend of mine—Donald Klein. He was like a brother to my husband, and when Dave passed away I don't know what I would have done if it hadn't been for Don. He watches over me. When he heard about all of the trouble we've been having he jumped in his car and drove all the way from Denver just to make sure I was all right."

Ben and Donald exchanged greetings, each warily sizing up the other.

"And what do you do?" Ben asked.

"I'm a retired university professor," Donald replied. "Keiler University in up state New York. Taught courses on world religions."

Donald seemed friendly enough, but it irked Ben to see him constantly hovering over Ann as if to protect her from the rest of the world.

"Hope you don't mind if our Irish friend here, Brady, rides along with us," Ben said to Ann. "He's my second shadow these days."

Brady, who had been lounging in the corner of the room, stepped forward to meet Donald. "I could have driven our hero to the funeral," Brady said, "but it might be better if I rode as a passenger where I can keep my eyes open."

Ann frowned at the implication that Ben might still be in danger. She gave him a long look, but said nothing.

There were a dozen people at the service. Besides Ben, Ann, Donald and Brady there were April Means and her husband, four other classmates that had stayed over for the service, and two FBI friends of Buddy's who had flown in from the east. Suzie had already returned to her office in Washington.

As Ben listened to the preacher who had been brought in for the occasion, a young man just out of seminary, he was overcome with a deep feeling of depression. It didn't seem right that Buddy would have so few people mourning him—Buddy, who had been one of the most popular boys in high school. And to have a service conducted by someone who didn't know Buddy from Adam. Several times the minister even had to refer to his notes to remember Buddy's name.

Buddy deserved better than this, Ben thought.

* * * * *

Two days later Ben was released from the hospital.

Ben and Brady were getting to be good friends, which was a good thing since Brady never left Ben's side. Brady decided it would be best to rent a car and drive back to Ben's home in Colorado rather than take the train. Brady did all of the driving, keeping a sharp eye on all of the other cars on the highway. He often would slow down to see if a car would pass them, or alternatively speed up to make sure a car behind them didn't do the same. Ben found it faintly amusing, but appreciated that Brady was taking his job seriously.

"Do you really think our terrorist buddy will come after me again?" Ben asked. "I've looked at all the pictures you guys showed me, and I've given my description to your artist. What more damage can I do?"

"Sure and you can identify him," Brady replied, "something nobody else can do. He may be somebody you might see some day out of the blue. Or if by the grace of God we should catch him, you can identify him in court. The bloody bloke just can't take the chance. I hate to say it, old buddy, but my bet is that he will try for you again."

Ben stared at the road without responding.

They took Interstate 10 across western Kansas and eastern Colorado. The late summer sun was warm, the scenery boring, and the miles long.

"Holy Mary, this is the most desolate land these Irish eyes have ever beheld," Brady said. "Where are the trees? Where is something green? There's not even a hill to lend a contrast to the land. And this is the Colorful Colorado I've been hearing so much about?"

"This is known as prairie, my lad," Ben replied. "Once home to the fearless Cheyenne Indians. And don't be deceived by the flat landscape. It's not really flat, but consists of gently rolling hills. Just looks flat. There are hidden ravines and small oases all over the place."

"My dear old Mother always told me that if it looks flat it is flat. It's a hard time you'll be having to convince me otherwise."

"Well, keep your eyes peeled. We ought to be able to spot the mountains off to the west anytime now. That's where the color in Colorful Colorado comes from."

Brady's cell phone rang, a short stanza from the music of When Irish Eyes Are Smiling. As soon as Brady answered, the features on his face softened, and a smile spread across his face. He talked in low tones, somewhat embarrassed in front of Ben. Ben tried not to listen, but knew that the call had to be from a girl friend. It was the third such call he had received since they had started the trip.

When Brady hung up, Ben said, "I don't mean to intrude on your personal business, but are these calls by any chance from a lady friend?"

"You trying to be a detective?" Brady asked, then added, "Don't know how you might have figured it out, but yes, they're from a lady friend. A pretty special lady friend."

"Well tell me this," Ben said, "how come she keeps calling you, but you never seem to call her?"

"It's a doctor she is. A medical doctor—an OB. Her schedule is pretty busy, never knows when she might be with a patient, so I let her call me when she's free."

Brady proceeded to tell Ben all about Sara. Obviously he was pretty smitten with the lady.

At Limon, Colorado they exited the Interstate, and filled up with gas at a truck stop. Brady examined all of the vehicles in the parking lot, but everything looked normal. When they went inside Brady stood to one side of the entrance and studied all of the customers. The truck stop was a large one, filled with souvenirs—Indian pottery, blankets, cowboy hats, cactus plants—and right in front of Brady were ten barrels, two rows of five each, filled with different flavors of salt water candy.

"Sure and would you look at that," Brady said. "My favorite candy laid out before me like dinner on a table."

"It's good taffy," Ben said. "Sometimes you find salt water taffy so hard it feels like a rock. These are nice and soft. Here—feel one." He handed one to Brady who molded it with his fingers.

"Sometimes it's terrible the decisions a man must make," Brady replied. "All of these flavors just waiting to be enjoyed. Which to pick? I think I will have to buy a few to test before I decide on the final selection."

When they left 30 minutes later Brady had a three pound sack of the delicacies clutched tightly in his hand and a satisfied smile on his face.

They took Highway 24 from Limon to Colorado Springs and then stayed on it as they headed into the mountains. On the way they stopped at a ranch just off the highway to pick up Ben's dog, Sadie, a Laboratory Retriever, from a neighbor who had been taking care of her while Ben was gone. Sadie was overjoyed to see Ben again, jumping on him and licking his face, her tail swinging wildly back and forth. Ben seemed equally happy to see Sadie.

Ben's house was on a gravel road about 1 mile south of the highway. It was a rambling one story ranch sitting on 40 acres of land, almost hidden by the thick stand of pine and blue spruce trees surrounding it. A small stream ran by the rear of the dwelling. The front of the residence faced towards Pikes Peak, which was beautifully framed by the picture window in the great room. The room itself, which was the center of the home, was huge, and had a rugged look to it, with aspen wood walls and vaulted ceiling. On one wall hung the mounted head of a brown bear, with mouth open and teeth glowing.

"I can see I'm going to enjoy this assignment," Brady remarked. "And did you be the one to shoot the bear?"

"Guess I have to plead guilty," Ben replied.

"So it's the great hunter you are then?"

"I used to be, way back in my long lost youth. But more recently I decided to do all of my wildlife shooting with a camera rather than a gun. The bear there was an exception—it was a matter of life and death—hers or mine. Mary and I had been out taking pictures and were camping in the woods near the base of Pike's Peak. During the night I heard something moving around outside of our tent, and got up to have a look. I always go into the woods armed, and had a revolver and deer rifle in the tent. I grabbed the rifle and went outside, and found myself face to face with Old Bessie there, as I call her."

"She took one look at me and came roaring straight in. I barely had time to get off one shot before she slammed into me, clawing my right shoulder, and sending me flying. I managed to hold on to the rifle however, and as she turned to have another go at me I fired four more shots into her while laying there on the ground. She rushed up to my feet, stopped, sagged for a minute, then fell over dead."

"Holy Jesus! You must have been scared out of your senses. How about Mary—was she hurt?"

"No. She had grabbed the revolver and came out after me, but was never able to get off a clear shot." Ben chuckled at the memory. "Probably a good thing 'cause she never was much of a marksman. If she had, chances are it might be my head hanging up there on the wall instead of Old Bessie."

"What made the beast come after you? I always thought bears would leave you alone if given a chance," Brady asked.

"Not really sure what set her off. I've always thought there must have been a cub around somewhere, but we never did find any trace of one."

Ben walked over to a gun case in the corner of the room, pulled out a key, and unlocked it. Inside were a 12 gauge shot gun, a 22 rifle, a Browning Bar 7 mm deer rifle, and two pistols.

Brady surveyed the arsenal before remarking, "Blessed Mary! A regular war cabinet you are having there."

"Thought I might as well unlock this just in case we have any need of them. We'll hope not. Only shots I want to take are with my camera."

The next several days were uneventful. Ben did all of the cooking, treating Brady to sourdough pancakes in the mornings, and fresh trout or venison steaks for dinner. They fished the streams, hiked the mountains, and chopped wood. The Aspen trees were in full color, and at times seemed to actually glow in the warm fall days. In the evenings they generally sat around the fireplace and talked, or listened to Ben's extensive collection of jazz favorites. Brady, who had never been a music enthusiast, decided that Coleman Hawkins—the Gilded Hawk—and his tenor sax were definitely OK. Ben's shoulder was improving rapidly.

One evening Brady asked Ben about Mary, about how happy they must have been judging by Ben's devotion.

"She was not a working woman I would guess," Brady commented.

"Guess it depends on your definition of 'working'," Ben replied. "In addition to being a full time mother, she was chief cook for the Foxworth family, teacher, counselor, housekeeper, bookkeeper, nurse, moral compass...."

"Alright already," Brady held up his hands. "Your point is well made. I meant she didn't have a profession outside of the family."

"No—her profession *was* the family. Why do you ask?"

"Oh, no reason. Sara, my girl friend is a doctor, you know."

"Yes—you've mentioned that a few hundred times, I believe. Does that bother you?"

"Sure and it makes me wonder just a wee bit. I've always thought a wife should be just like your Mary—a home maker. But Sara is committed to her job—doesn't intend to ever give it up. What kind of marriage would that be? I don't know if it would work having two professionals in the house. Who would raise our children?"

"Brady, I've known a lot of working couples, and they've managed a very happy and fulfilling marriage. Sure, it takes some adjustment on both sides, but when you truly love someone you want them to be everything they can be, as the Marines say. I know that you are proud of Sara, and you wouldn't want to do anything to stifle her dreams."

"That's exactly right, and I keep telling myself the very same thing. But still it worries me just a mite. We'd be eating out a lot for one thing, and I've yet to find a restaurant that knows how to make a good Irish stew."

Ben laughed, but could tell that the idea of having a professional wife really bothered Brady.

On the fourth evening after returning to Ben's home they settled down before the fireplace after an elk steak dinner, and as they sipped their evening cup of coffee, the conversation turned to Islam.

"I guess my picture of Muslims," Ben said, "is someone wrapped in a blanket and full of hate, intolerance and devoid of human compassion. And who have no respect for women's rights. Not someone who is a part of our society. Sour as he was, I have trouble seeing my old classmate, Gene Sawyer, in that light."

Brady laughed. "Although, 'tis really not a laughing matter, my lad. Your image comes close to the reality of Wahhabism, the cult that is trying to capture the religion and turn it into a justification for their own agenda of intolerance and violence. That is not the Islam that the vast majority of Muslims embrace."

"But how can this group stray so far from the rest of Islam?"

"The Wahhabis movement dates back to the 1800's. It was a small sect of plundering tribes in what is now Saudi Arabia that used Islam to justify thievery and cruelty to outsiders, and robbed Islam of its customary culture and beliefs. They forced their followers into a religion of submission and violence. It continues today, fostered by economic depression and hatred for all non-Muslims."

"But if true Islam practices tolerance and charity for others, as you have told me, how can these extremists claim to be any part of Islam?"

"Has not Christianity strayed from the true teachings of Jesus at times in the past? Look at the inquisition, the Crusades, witch trials in Salem. Did these truly represent the tenets of your faith as it is today? Any religion can be perverted by unscrupulous people to justify their own ends. And that is the battle that Islam faces."

"So what are the beliefs of the more accepted Muslim faith?"

"They believe in the same God, Allah, as you. But they believe that there is no God but God. No Father, Son and Holy Spirit as Christians believe. Jesus was a great prophet, but He was not God. His teachings were perfected by Mohammad, the last Prophet sent by God. They believe that one must honor his parents, respect the rights of others, be generous to those who are less fortunate, avoid killing except for justifiable causes, be humble and pure of heart—much of what Christians believe."

"I guess it's that 'avoid killing except for justifiable causes' that gets tricky," Ben replied. "It depends on what you consider a justifiable cause."

"Ah, but isn't that the same with Christians?"

Just then Sadie, who was lying in front of the fire, gave a low growl, and perked up her ears. She came to her feet, looked towards the door, and continued with a deep rumble in her throat. All of the drapes had been closed, so nobody from outside could see in.

Ben and Brady gave each other a warning look, and Brady pulled his Berretta 9mm revolver from his shoulder holster. Without a word Ben rose from his chair, dimmed the light, and walked over to the corner of the room to the gun cabinet. He removed a 12 gauge shot gun and loaded three shells into it. He stuffed more in his pants pocket.

For several minutes they were frozen in time, Sadie continuing to growl and stare at the door, Brady with gun pulled and standing in front of the fireplace, and Ben in the corner with the shot gun cradled in his arms. There was no other sound that the men could hear.

Then the unnatural quiet was broken as the glass in the picture window shattered with bullets erupting into the room from outside. Brady turned and fired rapidly through the drapes into the darkness beyond the window, and then fell to his knees with blood streaming down his shirt. Behind the curtains someone could be seen climbing through the window. His shoes were visible beneath the drapes. Brady managed to get off one last shot at him before falling forward, blood forming a pool beside his body.

A man in a dark pull-over sweater and dark pants, with a hood over his head, fell forward through the curtains, pulling them down as he fell. Brady had hit him through the heart, and he didn't move after he hit the floor. Ben heard the front door split open and two more hooded men raced into the room. Ben raised the shot gun and fired twice, blowing both men back into the doorway with gaping holes in their chests. Ben heard a rustling sound outside of the window and fired the third shell into the darkness of the night. He reloaded and raced to the front door, stepping over the two men who lay unmoving on the floor as he rushed outside.

In the bright moonlight he saw a man racing down the driveway towards a car parked a hundred yards up the road. He fired the shot gun again, but knew the range was too distant. Just outside of the shattered window he saw another man doubled up in the yard. Brady must have hit this one when he fired through the drapes. As he watched, the man managed to raise an arm with a pistol in it. He aimed it at Ben as Ben let loose with another blast from the shotgun. The result was devastating. Little was left of the man's head. It made Ben sick.

Ben returned to the room and rushed over to Brady's body. There was a lot of blood on the floor, but the wound didn't look life threatening. Ben went into the kitchen, grabbed some dish towels and raced back to where Brady lay. He pressed several of them tightly against the open wound to stop the bleeding, and then tied them into place with another.

As Ben finished with Brady he realized that Sadie wasn't by his side, which is where she normally would have been, wagging her tail and wanting to lick his face. He got up and looked carefully around the room. He saw her lying by the sofa in front of the window, inert and covered with blood. With a sinking heart Ben walked slowly over to the dog, and saw where the terrorist's bullets had slammed into her head.

The loss of Sadie seemed every bit as devastating as losing Buddy and John. Sadie was a faithful friend and companion, and had given Ben great comfort during the lonely evenings after his wife had died. A towering rage swept over Ben.

He checked the bodies of the three intruders who had been shot inside the house. None were alive. He studied their facial features carefully. All of the men appeared to be Mexican. Maybe they could be mid-eastern, but the shouts he had heard during the attack were definitely in Spanish. This struck Ben as exceedingly odd.

He knew there was no point in wondering about the man outside that he had shot at close range. He walked over to the telephone, picked it up, and called Bob Sager, the county sheriff, and a personal friend.

It was mid-morning before the bodies had been removed, and some semblance of order restored to the house. Brady had been rushed to the hospital, but not before he had talked with Sager and shown him his FBI badge. Together Sager, Brady and Ben had called Suzie Becker, Brady's partner, waking her at her apartment in Washington. Suzie assured Sager that this was a Federal matter, and that the FBI would be taking care of things.

The sheriff left one of his men with Ben, just in case there should be any further trouble. Ben cleaned up the room as best he could, called a contractor friend of his to come over the next day to replace the window and door, buried Sadie and fell into bed to sleep for a couple of hours.

When he awoke, he packed some things in a small overnight suitcase, told the deputy from the sheriff's office that he wasn't needed anymore, and called Susie.

"Susie, I'm taking off. I'm not sitting around here anymore waiting for more of the bad guys to come for me."

"Ben, you can't leave. I've got an FBI agent from Denver on his way to your place now. He'll take you to a safe house where the terrorists won't be able to find you. We should have done that to begin with. I didn't appreciate how badly they wanted you."

"Sorry, Suzie. I'm out of here. But one question. I thought we were dealing with just three Anglo terrorists—two with Sawyer out of the picture. Last night there were five guys after me. And they were all Hispanic. Where in Hell did they come from?"

"I don't honestly know, Ben. I guess there is more than one terrorist cell here in the country, and they communicate with each other. Are you sure they were Hispanic, not mid-eastern? I would guess the men who came after you last night were borrowed from another cell. But the three Anglos, or two now, are still the ones who are number one on our list. We've got to get them before they pull off their next attack. Our sources tell us that it will be something very dramatic and deadly."

"Good luck, Suzie. I'll be in touch."

"Ben Foxworth! You stay right where you are. You can't leave. Do you hear me?"

"I hear you lady. But I've got things to do and places to go. These thugs have killed two of my best friends, shot my dog, tore up my house, and tried to kill me twice now. I'm not going to just sit around and wait for them to come back."

"Where are you going, Ben? At least tell me where you are going."

"Sorry, Suzie. If I did that it wouldn't be a secret anymore. Who knows—my telephone is probably tapped. I'll call you later."

"Ben—"

He placed the telephone back in the receiver, picked up his bags, and left. In Colorado Springs he stopped at the bank, withdrew $5,000, and proceeded to the Memorial Hospital, where Brady had been taken. Brady was sleeping, but the nurse assured Ben that he was doing just fine, and would probably be released in a few days. Ben placed a sack on the stand near the bed—a sack filled with the salt water taffy Brady had purchased in Limon—or what was left of it—and silently thanked Brady for protecting him at the cost of almost losing his own life. He left the hospital and headed for the airport.

CHAPTER NINE

Ben's first stop was Chicago. After departing the plane he went to the American Airways ticket counter and booked a flight to New York, leaving at 6:00 that evening. He paid cash for the ticket. He had read how a person can be traced fairly rapidly—within a day or two—when using a credit card, and he didn't want to give his New York destination away to anyone—even the FBI. That was why he hadn't scheduled a flight directly to the big city from Colorado Springs.

He checked his watch. It was 11:00 a.m., giving him roughly five hours till he needed to be back. He pulled an address book from his coat pocket, and looked up John's telephone number, which he had gotten from his old friend back in Oldvil. He freed his cell phone from his belt, looked at it a moment, and then returned it to its case. *I guess they can track these things, too*, he thought. He found a telephone booth in the terminal and dialed John's number.

A woman answered on the third ring.

"This is Ben Foxworth," he said. "I am calling for Beth Wilkerson."

There was a slight pause before she answered. "This is she."

"Hi, Beth. You probably don't know who I am, but John and I went to high school together. We were great friends."

"Yes, I know who you are. John spoke often of you in these past few weeks. He was looking forward to seeing you again at the reunion."

"And the same here. I am in town—just passing through—and wondered if I could stop by for a few minutes this afternoon. I would very much like to meet you, and tell you how much John meant to me. Which may sound strange, seeing as how John and I haven't talked to each other in around forty years. But we were very close in high school, and after we got together again in Oldvil, I realized how much he had helped to shape my life when we were growing up."

"I would be very happy to meet you, Ben. The police in Oldvil have not been overly informative about what happened to John. Just the bare essentials, I guess. I would like to hear about everything that happened at the reunion."

Beth gave Ben instructions on how to reach her house. He went out of the airport, hailed a cab, and 45 minutes later was there.

It was a two-story brick house in a neighborhood of brick homes. At the front of the residence five steps led up to a screened-in front porch. Several bushes and flowers, mostly petunias, lined the front of the porch on each side of the entrance. Before Ben could press the doorbell he heard barking—or more accurately yelping—from inside. Obviously a small dog. A few seconds later the front door opened and a slim woman approached the screen door to the porch, carrying a tan Pomeranian with ears on high and still growling softly. She was attractive, Ben thought, with graying hair, clear hazel eyes and a small turned up nose. But her smile seemed to highlight the grief that was still written on her face.

"You must be Ben," she said as she opened the door. "Come on in. Brownie here won't bite. He's all bark and no action," She placed the dog on the floor. Brownie still wasn't too sure about Ben, and had to come up and smell his pants leg. He apparently passed the test because Brownie seemed to accept him and didn't bark any more.

The entrance opened to a living room, but Beth led them to a table in the kitchen area. "I've taken the liberty of making some sandwiches. I forgot to ask if you had eaten already."

"Matter of fact I haven't," Ben replied. "Sandwiches sound good."

They talked for over two hours. Ben told her—somewhat sheepishly—about their water balloon encounter with Gene Sawyer, about learning that Sawyer was a suspected terrorist, about his finding Buddy's body, and the next night about John. He described his own assault at the motel, but didn't discuss the most recent events in Colorado. Beth had many questions about John's last few days, making Ben glad that he had come to see her and pay his respects.

"I just can't seem to understand it all," Beth said. "John being killed by terrorists is about the last thing I would ever have been able to imagine. How can there be so much hatred and violence in the world? And it appears that all of this is now happening right here in our own back yard, not somewhere across the ocean."

Ben wasn't able to answer her question. A growing anger consumed him as he thought about everything that had happened. *I'm going to do everything I can to bring these murders to justice*, he thought. *I owe it to Buddy and John. And John's family.*

"And the police don't have any idea who the killer is?" Beth asked.

"We know what he looks like," Ben replied. "That's why John was killed and an attempt made on my life. I promise you, Beth, that one way or another we will find this man and bring him to justice. I won't rest until we do."

Beth smiled and placed her hand over Ben's, but she didn't seem to exude any confidence that it would ever happen.

A car horn sounded from outside, and Ben checked his watch. Three o'clock. He had instructed the cabbie that brought him here to arrange for a taxi to pick him up. Ben rose and made his goodbyes to Beth, assuring her once again that the killer would be found and dealt with.

* * * * *

The plane was only a few minutes late as it landed at La Guardia Airport. It was dark when Ben took a taxi into town. He told the cab driver he wanted a hotel near the Bamford Law School. Fortunately the cabbie knew where the school was located, and delivered Ben to a mid-class resident hotel just a block away from the institution.

Once again Ben paid for the room with cash rather than using his credit card. *I guess I'm being overly cautious,* he thought. *I probably won't be here that long anyway.* Ben wasn't sure where he would go from here. He had tried to sound confident that the FBI would find the killer when he was talking with Beth, but now he wasn't so sure. This trip was undoubtedly a waste of time, but it was either go on the run, or check into the safe house Suzie had promised. He preferred being out on his own. He thought briefly about visiting his daughter in Washington, but quickly decided that wasn't a good idea. He didn't intend to place anyone else in harm's way. And time was running out. He had to feel like he was doing something even if it was futile.

The next morning he rose early and had breakfast at a small restaurant half way between the hotel and the Law School. As he ate he thought about the pictures Suzie had shown him from Sawyer's graduating class. None of them had looked anything like the man they had seen leaving Sawyer's house that fateful afternoon. But if the man was linked to Sawyer through the law school, it didn't necessarily have to be someone actually in his class. It could be a student in the classes ahead of him, or someone behind him. Ben wanted to look at the pictures of all students who might have been in the institution during the three years Sawyer was there.

When he finished with his breakfast, he got up, paid the bill, and went outside. On the way to the law school he detoured a few blocks to the east to look at the mosque Suzie and Brady had told him about. The place where Sawyer might have been indoctrinated into terrorism. Brady had told him that this mosque had been taken over by the Whahabis. The funding came from Saudi Arabia, and the sermons from the Inmans were revolutionary and promoted violence, but they were careful to stay within the limits of the law. The place of worship looked quiet and serene in the morning sun.

Ben knew from having looked it up on the Internet several days before that the building was built at a slight diagonal from the street so that it would face towards Mecca. The structure itself was three stories high with a large dome on the top. Ben suspected that there were no second or third levels inside, however, only an open room with the extra height providing a spacious area for prayer. The walls at the third level were ornate glass which would allow bright sunlight into the prayer chamber. Next to the mosque was a minaret, a tall, slim structure from which the faithful would be called to prayer in Muslim countries.

Ben watched the people entering and leaving the mosque. Some of the women were wearing full length bright colored dresses extending down to their ankles, some with dresses to just below the knees with slacks underneath, and some in modern attire. All had a scarf or shawl over their heads, however. Most of the men wore suits or working clothes.

Ben knew that Muslims prayed five times each day: just before sunrise, immediately after noon, late in the afternoon, at dusk and sometime after dark. The people leaving the mosque probably had been there for the morning prayer—the *Fajr* as they called it. Ben had been doing a lot of reading about Muslims after he got home from Oldvil. He had been surprised to learn that the first Muslim church in America had been built in Cedar Rapids, Iowa, in 1934. He wouldn't have thought the first mosque in this country would be in the heart of the Bible country. But there had been a rapid expansion of the religion. Now in New York City alone there were over 100 mosques.

When the front door opened Ben could see a rack containing shoes of the worshipers just inside. They apparently took them off upon entering the mosque and placed them on the shelves. Ben thought about going over and asking if he could visit inside the building. He had read that American Muslims welcomed visitors, but he decided against it. Probably should make an appointment ahead of time, not just walk in off the street.

He pulled his cell phone from the case clipped onto his belt, and called his daughter in Seattle. A sleepy voice answered.

"Hello—who is this?"

"Hi Beth. Time to rise and shine."

"Dad—what's wrong? Why are you calling so early?"

"Early? It's almost 8:00 o'clock. Time all decent folk were up and tending to chores."

"Eight o'clock? I don't know where you are but it's only 5:00 here. Come to think of it, where are you? Not at home I take it."

"Well, at the moment I'm sitting on a bench at a bus stop in New York, watching the New Yorkers go about their early morning business. I've gotten tangentially involved in an interesting case and I'm back here doing a little research at a law school," he explained.

Ben and his daughter chatted for another 15 minutes, but Ben didn't tell her about the attack at his home. Once again Beth tried to convince Ben to sell his home in Colorado and move to Seattle.

"Something could happen and no one would even know. You could slip on the ice some morning and break a hip, and you'd just lay there and freeze to death. And what are you doing on a case? I thought you were retired, and anyway you are supposed to be home recuperating."

"Whoa—one thing at a time," Ben pleaded. "If I fell on the ice you would know almost immediately if you called me every day like a dutiful daughter should, and you always tell me I should keep occupied with some project or another, and sitting on a bus bench isn't hurting my shoulder one little bit."

When they finally hung up Ben watched the worshippers enter and leave the mosque for another 10 minutes, then walked up the street to a five story, brick building that must have been built over 100 years ago. The structure seemed in good shape in spite of its age. There was a large sign over the main entrance announcing that this was the Bamford School of Law. Students were streaming in and out of ten foot high double doors.

Ben walked into the lobby and saw a young woman sitting behind an information desk reading a book. It was a massive work on Business and Corporate Litigation. *Must be a student*, Ben thought. He waited impatiently at the desk for a full minute before she looked up. "Can I help you?" she finally inquired, seeming somewhat annoyed at being disturbed.

"Yes, if you would be so kind. I went to school here back in the 50's. There was a student acquaintance of mine back then that I would like to get in touch with, but for the life of me I can't remember his last name. I was thinking that if you had year books for that time, I might find his picture with his name in it. It was Mike something."

"Check the Library. Fifth floor," the woman replied and went back to her book.

If she's a law student, Ben thought, *she's going to be giving us lawyers a bad name.* Then he chuckled to himself. *As if we needed any worse name than we already have.* Nevertheless he thanked her graciously, found the elevator, and proceeded to the top floor.

The librarian there was more helpful, and showed Ben to a shelf that contained all of the old yearbooks. Ben remembered Sawyer telling him that he had graduated in 1958, so to start with he pulled the publications for 1956 and 1957 from the shelf. As an after thought he also pulled the book for 1955, even though the law school was only a three year course. He took these to a table, and carefully studied the pictures of each graduating class. He found one student in the class of 1956 who conceivably could fit the description of the mystery man, although it took a stretch of the imagination. Nevertheless, he jotted down the man's name. Other than that, nothing.

He returned these books to the shelf, and took down the ones for 1959, 1960 and 1961. Several hours later he sat by the table, totally dejected. He had really thought he might be able to come up with something from his search, but after looking at all of the students he hadn't found any that truly resembled the man they were searching for. The one name he had written down hadn't really looked much like him either, Ben decided. He tore the paper up, tossed it in the wastepaper basket, and wondered what he should do now. Go back to Denver and the safe house Suzie had promised?

He was still in a rage over all that had happened. The whole affair had become very personal for him. It just wasn't in his nature to sit back and do nothing. The thought of hiding in some FBI house did not appeal to him one bit. He would rather be in the open as a decoy to try to bring the terrorists out. Maybe he should suggest this to Suzie.

He returned the yearbooks to the shelf, and idly pulled Sawyer's class book out and thumbed through it. These were the pictures Suzie had shown him when he was in the hospital. And there was good old Gene, smiling broadly and looking very pleased with himself. Just as he closed the book a picture on the last page jumped out at him.

He reopened the book and turned to the back. There it was! That was him! Ben felt a surge of excitement. Was that really him? A small doubt crept into his mind, but as he studied the picture again he was sure that this was the mystery man. The face was, of course, much younger than the man Ben had seen, and at this stage in his life didn't show much in the way of character development. No lines around the eyes or corners of the mouth, and much more innocent looking. But it was the same face, Ben would bet on it.

But why had this picture not been in the group Suzie had shown him of Sawyer's classmates? Looking more closely at the yearbook, Ben saw that Sanchez had not graduated at the same time as the rest of the class. He and a half dozen others had finished in September of that year. Suzie, or whoever had gotten the pictures for her, must have missed him for that reason.

Sloppy work, Suzie, he thought to himself.

The name below the picture indicated that the face belonged to Anthony Sanchez, from Las Vegas, New Mexico. The name had a familiar ring to it, but Ben couldn't think where he might have heard it. He looked around for the librarian and saw her busy putting some books on the shelf on the other side of the room. Quickly he tore the picture of Sanchez out of the book, stuffed it in his shirt pocket, and returned the book to the shelf.

The library had a few computers on tables spread around the room. Ben hurried over to one, and sat down in front of it, hoping that it might be connected to the Internet, and not just to a local library system. He was in luck. Once on the Internet, he typed in Sanchez's name, hoping that he might have a web page somewhere. Most lawyers did.

Ben was surprised at the number of hits that his request generated. Sanchez was a popular name. But within minutes he discovered that the Anthony Sanchez he had seen in Oldvil was now the Attorney General for New Mexico. There were pictures of him, a little fuzzy and indistinct, but once again Ben thought they looked exactly like his man. More recent articles indicated that Sanchez was running for the Senate seat being vacated by New Mexico's senior senator, and looked like a good bet to win. Ben remembered now where he had heard Sanchez's name. It had been on CNN when he was in the hospital.

Reading through Sanchez's web page, Ben learned that Sanchez was making a campaign appearance in the town square in Old Town, Albuquerque three days from now. That would be a perfect opportunity to get a close-up look at the man, Ben thought, and to decide if it really was the same person he had seen leaving Sawyer's house. He needed to know for certain if this was his man. He had seen too many careers ruined by accusations that had subsequently turned out to be in error, but by then the damage had been done.

Ben hurried back to his hotel room, checked out, and took a cab to the airport. He bought a ticket for a flight that was leaving that evening for Albuquerque.

He called Suzie before boarding.

"Suzie, I think I've found our man. Anthony Sanchez, Attorney General for New Mexico and running for the Senate in Washington."

"What? Ben—where are you?"

"I'm at the airport at LaGuardia. I'm about to catch a plane to Albuquerque. I think I've found him, Suzie. I went to Bamford Law School and checked the yearbooks—Sanchez didn't graduate in the spring like everyone else. He was one of six people who graduated in September. That's probably how you missed him."

"Ben, what are you talking about? You think this Anthony Sanchez is the man that was visiting Gene Sawyer?"

"That's right. I couldn't swear to it in a court of law just based on the photos, but I'm on my way to Albuquerque to see him in person to make sure."

"Ben—you are to do no such thing. Do you hear me? I want you to return to Colorado right this minute, and contact the FBI office in Denver. You are not to go anywhere near this Sanchez. I will contact our office in Albuquerque to check him out. This is FBI business, and I don't want a civilian running around screwing things up. You are to steer clear of Sanchez. I mean it, Ben. And you are not to say a word of this to anyone. Not one person."

"I read you, Suzie. I'll be in touch."

Ben pocketed his cell phone with Suzie still reading him the riot act, and proceeded to the boarding gate for the flight to Albuquerque.

On the plane Ben remembered that this was the week that Ann and her friends were going to Albuquerque for the International Balloon Festival. He tried to think of the name of the hotel at which they were staying. Casas something. It was located in Old Town. Casas de Suenos. That was it.

When the plane unloaded in Albuquerque, Ben called the Casas de Suenos to see if they had a vacancy. The clerk sounded somewhat amused that Ben would think they would have any openings during the balloon festival. Ben ended up calling five motels before he found a Best Western on the north end of town that had just had a cancellation. The price was outrageous, but Ben took it.

It was well past midnight before Ben found the motel, settled in for the night, and crashed in the bed, exhausted.

CHAPTER TEN

In the morning Ben called Ann at the Casas de Suenos.
"Hi, Ann. Ben Foxworth. How's the balloon festival going?"
"Ben! The balloons are wonderful—everything I had expected. Where are you?"
"Here in Albuquerque. Came down on some personal business. I wondered if you might like to take a little drive this afternoon, see some of the New Mexico fall color, and have dinner at one of my favorite restaurants."
"Oh, Ben. I would love to, but I've already promised Donald Kline—you remember him—you met him in Oldvil at John's funeral—I've already promised him that we'd go out tonight. All of the rest of our group are going to the balloon moon glow this evening, but Don and I thought we'd rather have a nice relaxing evening away from the crowds."
"Good luck on the crowds," Ben replied, trying to keep the disappointment out of his voice. "But bring him along. The more the merrier."
"Where did you have in mind?" Ann asked.
"A little village above Santa Fe—Chimayo. There's an old Spanish mission there I think you'd enjoy seeing."
"Ben, that sounds wonderful. I'm sure Don would love to go. Do you have a car?"

"Yup. Or I will have. How about I pick you both up around 3:00?"

"It's a date," Ann said. "Is your Irish bodyguard with you?"

"No. It's a long story, but he's resting up from his arduous assignment."

"I take it that that is good news. See you this afternoon."

Ben decided not to mention his suspicions about Sanchez to anyone and his real reason for being here. He wanted to be absolutely sure before he made any accusations. Especially for a man running for public office.

Later that day, as they headed out of Santa Fe, with Ann in the front seat and Donald in the rear, Ben told them about the mission at Chimayo.

"It all started around 1810," he said. "Seems like a Catholic friar was doing penances up in the valley when he saw a strange light on the hillside. He began digging on the spot and unearthed a large crucifix. He had it taken to his church in Santa Cruz, but three different times it disappeared, and each time was found back in the hole from which it had been dug. The friar realized that the crucifix of Our Lord of Esquipulas, as it is called, didn't want to be hauled off somewhere else. It wanted to remain on the hillside on which it was discovered. So a small chapel was built on the spot."

"Remarkable," Donald said. "Now I remember reading about this place. I taught religion at the university, you know."

"I remember," Ben replied. "But that's not the end of the story. Shortly after the chapel was built, people began experiencing miraculous healings. That drew so many of the faithful that in 1816 they had to build a larger chapel. That's the one that is still standing, and is still active today. The crucifix is on the altar. There's a Prayer Room next to the chapel that is filled with discarded crutches and before-and-after pictures of those who have been cured at the spot. The people began to think that the healing powers came from the sand and dirt in which the crucifix had been buried. So just off the chapel is a tiny cubical with a hole in the floor from which people can scoop up small sacks of the miraculous healing sand. They take it home, and sprinkle it on their food when they are in need of healing."

"Ben, what a wonderful legend," Ann said.

"Well, I'm not sure 'legend' is the right word. Every year at Easter hundreds of people make a pilgrimage from Albuquerque and Santa Fe on foot to pay homage to El Santuario de Chimayo, many crawling on their knees the last few yards. I think they would consider the story more than just a legend."

"This is wonderful," Donald said. "I never dreamed when we set out that we'd be in for such a grand trip. Positively wonderful."

Ben turned off of Highway 84 onto state road 503 a few miles north of Santa Fe. "If we had turned the other way on this road we'd have been heading up the mountain to Los Alamos, birth place of the atomic bomb," Ben said.

"What a contrast," Donald mused. "Atomic bombs to kill people, and missionary chapels to heal them."

As they proceeded the terrain surrounding the two lane road became bleak and barren. Rolling hills of rock and sand, with almost nothing growing. There were few cars.

"By God, this is the most desolate land I have ever laid eyes on," Donald said. "You mean pilgrims walk all this way to Chimayo? Through this wasteland?"

"That they do," Ben replied. "If you watch along the road you will see crosses occasionally that the pilgrims left to guide the way. But wait till you see what is at the end."

As he spoke, they came over the crest of one of the hills and immediately were in a green, lush valley. The beautiful village of Chimayo.

"The Garden of Eden," Donald muttered, as he looked around in wonder.

"Amazing how a stream can turn infertile land into a virtual paradise," Ben said.

After spending an hour at the chapel, Ben took them to El Rancho de Chimayo for dinner. The rear of the restaurant was in the open and backed onto a small hill which had been terraced with tables on each level looking down on the main floor. A Mariachi band wandered through the premises playing Mexican music.

As they sipped their margaritas Ann touched Ben's hand and said, "Ben, this has been one of the most wonderful days I've had for a long, long time. Thanks so much for bringing us."

Ben felt a pleasant sensation spread through his body at her touch, but then scowled at Donald who was vigorously stirring his drink.

On the way back to Albuquerque, to Ben's dismay, Ann insisted on sitting in the back seat so Donald and Ben 'could visit.' But it was Ann who was suddenly full of questions.

"Ben, we've had such a busy day and everything at Oldvil seems so far away. But where is your body guard—the FBI agent? Brady Jones, was that his name? I thought he was going to stick with you till all the danger was past. Does that mean they've caught the killer?"

Ben hesitated, wondering just how much he should say. "Well, I think it's mostly all over," he said. "They did make another attempt at my home in Colorado, but most of the bad guys were turned away. Brady took a bullet in the process, though, and is in the hospital in the Springs. I don't think they'll try anything again," he lied.

"Who's this 'they'," Donald said. "I thought it was just one guy—or maybe two."

"Seems like they had a few others they could call in," Ben replied. "But I think they've decided that it's unlikely I would ever identify the guy we saw leaving Sawyer's. Not likely I'll ever run into him again."

Ann didn't look convinced, but said nothing more.

"Nasty business all the way around, if you ask me," Donald said.

"So you taught religion at the university," Ben said to Donald, anxious to change the subject. "Any one religion in particular?"

"Oh no," Donald replied. "All of them. There is a certain universality across all beliefs. And they all present a code of conduct for people to live by. Main difference I sometimes think is how seriously people take them. In this country, for instance, everyone is relatively prosperous, so who needs God? The truly faithful are the poor souls in need. Here we have become complacent. And we support a country, Israel, over the millions of Muslims struggling in the mid-east. Not surprising that we were attacked at the World Trade Center. To a certain extent one might say we deserved it."

Ben studied Donald closely. "You aren't one of those who think all the people killed in that attack had blood on their hands, are you? That there are no innocents?"

"No—I wouldn't go quite that far. But to the extent that we, as a nation, ignore the suffering of the underprivileged in this world, I would say that there are no innocents."

"I believe," Ben said, "that anyone who thinks those men, women and children deserved to die must be crazy."

The rest of the trip home was spent mostly in silence.

CHAPTER ELEVEN

Ben was up early the next morning. He worked out for 45 minutes in the motel's exercise room, and then had a waffle and orange juice in the breakfast room. His shoulder was still a little stiff, but seemed to be healing nicely.

When he stepped outside he was greeted by the "whoooom" sound of gas being ignited in a hot air balloon. Looking up he saw the grinning face of Mickey Mouse, large ears flopping in the morning breeze, only 50 yards above him. The four occupants seemed to be having a great time, waving to the spectators below as they passed by. Other balloons filled the morning sky, making a kaleidoscope of color against the deep blue of the atmosphere. A number of them were special shapes like Mickey. There was the face of a black and white Panda Bear, an old tennis shoe, and a pink dinosaur with tongue licking the brisk morning air.

One of the men standing near him remarked, "Must not have had the box affect this morning that would allow them to stay near the launch area. These are drifting right on down the Rio Grande River bed. Sure does make a beautiful sight."

Ben agreed.

By 9:00 he was in Albuquerque's Old Town where Sanchez was scheduled to give a campaign appearance in another hour. He parked his rented car in a small parking lot just to the east of the town plaza, and strolled leisurely along the streets lined with souvenir shops featuring Native and southwestern collectibles. A few Indians had already spread their blankets on the sidewalk on the east side of the plaza, displaying their wares of silver, pottery and weaving. Ben knew this was a tradition started in 1706, the only restriction being that the vendors had to be Indian and the wares had to be hand made by the natives.

A wedding was taking place at the San Felipe Catholic Mission on the north of the plaza. The wedding party had arrived, the men dressed in formal attire, and the bride's maids decked out in bright colorful dresses. The church had been in continuous use for over 300 years, and was listed in the National Register for Historical Properties.

At 9:30 two vans pulled up on the south side of the plaza. Three men emerged and began setting up folding chairs in front of the rotunda in the center of the plaza. They placed a sound system in front of the stage along with placards urging people to vote for Anthony Sanchez for Senator.

Ben hung around on the sidewalk across from the plaza, waiting for Sanchez to appear. At precisely five minutes before ten, a black Mercedes pulled up, and Anthony Sanchez and his close advisors emerged. Sanchez strode purposely up to the rotunda, tested the loud speakers briefly, and then sat down on the chairs arranged on the platform. At 10:00 sharp his associates began playing Spanish music on the sound system. A small crowd began to gather in front of the podium, some sitting in the folding chairs to listen to the music.

Ben wandered over to the plaza just as the music ended and Sanchez rose to the microphone and began to speak. He was a slender man with a dark complexion, a sharp nose and straight black hair combed to the back of his head. A small shiver went through Ben as he studied the man's face. There was no doubt about it. This was the man he had seen leaving Gene Sawyer's house in Oldvil.

As Sanchez talked about his qualifications for the Senate, and what he would do if elected, his eyes fell on Ben. Sanchez paused momentarily, a look of recognition crossing his face. *Uh oh*, Ben thought, *He recognizes me. I'd better high tail it out of here.*

Ben moved slowly to the edge of the small crowd, trying not to attract attention, and then took off for his car. He failed to notice the sign Sanchez gave to two of his associates who hastily left the stage and followed. One was a large beefy man with pockmarks covering his face, and the other a thin man with a face like a weasel and a thin black mustache. The two caught up with Ben just as he reached his car and started to unlock it.

"You will come with us, senor," the Weasel said, displaying a small revolver aimed at Ben's stomach. "It is of little matter to me whether I kill you here, or take you for a talk with our leader. Of course, it will be better for you to come for this talk."

Ben hesitated, considering his options. He scanned the parking lot for possible help, but there was no body in sight. He had little choice.

The two took Ben to their own car parked in the same lot and the beefy man pushed Ben roughly into the back seat. "You will lie down in the seat, Senor Foxworth," the thin one said, "and you will not raise your head or make a sound or I will take it as a sign that you no longer wish to live. As I say, it is of little importance to me one way or the other."

The car moved out of the parking lot, and within minutes increased to a high speed. Ben could tell they were on an interstate. They drove for several hours before slowing for another town. Lying on the back seat Ben was able to see the tops of buildings as they passed. One was a sign for the Taos Hacienda

Inn. Ben had spent many vacations here, and knew the area well. That meant that they must have taken the by-pass around Santa Fe and now were in the picturesque and old village of Taos. Leaving town they drove for another 30 minutes, the last 10 of which were on a bumpy, dusty road. The car came to a halt and Ben was allowed to sit up. They were in front of an adobe ranch building, with stables and bunk houses about 40 yards in the rear. No other buildings were in site. Ben spotted a dozen men lounging around the stable.

The Weasel and Beefy hustled Ben out of the car and into the house. The vestibule opened to a large great room. At the front end of the room there was a brown, leather sofa with two end chairs, and a coffee table made of oak, facing a large fireplace to the right. At the rear of the hall there was a large dining table with eight chairs. All of the furnishings were of Spanish decor. A hallway ran to the right of the vestibule with several doors opening onto it. The men pushed Ben down the hall, which turned to the left at the corner of the house and continued to a room at the rear of the building. Ben was pushed into the small area, which had only a single, barred window high on the wall, and a single overhead light. The only furniture was a bunk bed.

"You will now wait, Senor, for our benefactor to come," the Weasel said. "He wishes to talk with you about certain things." With that he slammed the door shut and locked it from the outside.

Ben climbed onto the cot and tested the window. The bars were solid. From the window he could see the bunk houses and men at the back of the house. Ben sat down on the bed and considered his position. It was definitely not good. Sanchez had already tried to kill him twice. There was no way Ben would be allowed to leave this place alive.

Ben's thoughts turned to his wife, Mary, and their daughter. Theirs had been a good life, he thought. Full of love and commitment to each other. A feeling of contentment swept over him. As he thought about his life—his youth, his marriage with Mary, raising Beth, his law practice—it seemed that everything that had happened was just one extended journey. A trip that began with birth and now would end with death when he would return home—wherever and whatever that home might be. He was suddenly overwhelmed by a longing to complete this journey and to see Mary and all of his old friends again. He did not fear what might lie ahead.

But one thing he resolved. He wouldn't go out with a whimper. He would fight it all the way. *I'll leave this life the way I came in*, he thought. *Kicking and screaming.*

Eventually he fell asleep for a few hours, awaking to the sound of voices outside of his room. Glancing at the window he saw it was turning dark.

A key rattled in the lock, and the door swung open, revealing the Weasel with pistol in hand. "You will come now, Senor."

Ben was ushered down the hall to a door just this side of the great room, which opened to a study where Sanchez was sitting behind a massive oak desk. There were two overstuffed leather chairs in front of the desk, a table with a bouquet of flowers to the right, and a closet door to the left.

"Come in, Mr. Foxworth. As you have already discerned, we have been expecting you. I knew it was only a matter of time before you discovered my identity. The disadvantage of being a politician. Please, have a seat."

Ben sat in an overstuffed chair in front of the desk. The Weasel stood behind him with gun still in hand.

"Welcome to one of my unofficial offices," Sanchez said. "You will forgive the rather unorthodox way I have invited you to this place, but you will understand that it is imperative that I know everyone with whom you have talked and what you might have said. Sadly, it is a question of whether I must disappear into Mexico, or whether I can continue with the career I have worked so hard to obtain."

"You mean your career of killing innocent people?" Ben asked. "And I understand you have another terrorist assignment just ahead of you. When is it due?"

"In a few weeks now. But I don't discuss these things, even in front of my most trusted servants. As you have probably surmised I am the one that was forced to eliminate your Mr. Callahan and that friend of his, the other FBI agent. And I sent my men to deal with you a week ago at your home. A pity they failed. The question now is how many others know that you have succeeded in identifying me?" As he talked, Sanchez rose from his chair, moved around to the front of the desk, and leaned against it.

"I guess I can help you there," Ben replied. "The FBI know all about you. In fact they are probably on their way here right now. Killing me will not help you. I'd advise that you waste no time crossing the border if that is your intent."

"Ah, that is very helpful," Sanchez said. "The FBI of course. And who else? But there is a slight problem, you see. I don't believe that I can rely on everything you tell me, at least voluntarily. And as you have just stated, I have little time to waste, so we must resort to the help of a few chemicals. Ramos," Sanchez said to the Weasel, "there is a small bag on the top shelf of the closet. Will you be so kind as to retrieve it for me?"

The Weasel moved to the closet and opened the door. The shelf was high, higher than he could reach. With a quick look at Ben, he laid the revolver on a table next to the door, and pulled a folding footstool from the closet, opened it and climbed up two steps to reach the leather bag. Sanchez meanwhile continued talking, caught up in his own rhetoric as much as for Ben's benefit.

"There are some who doubt the effectiveness of this drug—Sodium Pentothal—but I have been able to get a very potent strain from the Russians who have become rather experienced in this area," Sanchez continued. "I believe they refer to it as SP-17. It was used with great effectiveness on the Russian defector Alexander Litvinenko."

Ben realized it must be now or never. Sanchez was engrossed in his own monologue like a true politician, and the Weasel was still at the top of the footstool reaching for the bag. Ben clutched the ends of the chair, and without warning, flung himself forward and across the room to where the Weasel's gun lay on the table. Sanchez was so startled that it took him a moment to respond with a yell of warning.

As Ben shot across the room the Weasel turned on the footstool to see what was happening. With a grunt he dropped the satchel and leapt from the stool, landing beside the stand and picked up the revolver. But before he could raise it all the way Ben crashed into him, grabbing the Weasel's gun arm with one hand and the barrel of the revolver with the other. They smashed against the closet door and the pistol fired. Ben felt an excruciating pain in his shoulder and was suddenly covered with warm, sticky blood. As they fell to the floor Ben felt the Weasel's grip on the gun go slack and then Ben had the weapon in both of his hand. Lying on the floor he twisted around, seeing that Sanchez had run around to the back of the desk and was pulling a revolver out of the front drawer. Ben fired, and Sanchez staggered, still clutching the gun. He looked dazed but tried to raise the weapon with shaking hands. Ben fired again, and Sanchez fell back behind the desk.

At that instant the door to the hall flew open and Beefy burst into the room. It took him a minute to size up the situation, and before he could act Ben fired two shots into his chest. Beefy slumped to his knees, knelt there a moment, then fell flat on his face.

Ben examined himself to see how bad the wound might be, and realized that he had not been hit. The blood that covered his face was from the Weasel. The bullet had entered Ramos' lower jaw, angled up through his mouth into his skull, and out the top of his head. The pain in Ben's shoulder was from his old wound, which throbbed from smashing into the Weasel.

Ben leaped to his feet and hurried to the door, pausing to pick up Beefy's pistol as he stepped over the body. He ran to the vestibule and out the front door. The Ford Mustang was sitting where they had parked it that morning, and behind it a Toyota pickup, which Sanchez must have driven. Ben rushed to the car, opened the door and looked for keys. There were none. He then checked the pick-up, but there were no keys there either. *Damn,* He thought, *I should have looked for keys in Beefy's pocket.*

He started back to the house but saw a dozen men pouring out of the bunk houses, shouting and pointing in his direction. They had heard the shots and were rushing to the ranch house. Most carried rifles or small arms. Two of the men were already nearing the rear entrance. Turning, Ben ran past the vehicles and into the desert.

The moon was almost full, lighting the night as if it were still twilight. *So much for the cover of darkness,* Ben thought. He could see his shadow as he ran. There was not a lot of cover—a few mesquite trees, sage brush and yucca cactus.

A cry rose from the house. The two men had discovered the bodies, and the group was now after him in earnest, shouting to each other in Spanish. Then Ben heard the unmistakable crack of a rifle, then of another. As he sprinted over the top of a slight hill he sensed the splat of a bullet smashing into the ground just to his right. He looked back and could see the men were gaining on him rapidly. Ben was in good shape for a 68 year old man, but he realized that this was a race he would not win.

He ran in a zigzag direction, trying to keep clumps of brush and trees between himself and his pursuers. The bright moonlight lit up the desert like stage lights, Ben thought. Soon he realized he was going uphill as his breath became more labored and his heart felt like it was going to burst right out of his rib cage. He stole a quick look back at his pursers and saw that they were gaining on him rapidly. He knew he couldn't keep going at this pace. He heard another sharp crack of a rifle and was sure that he could sense the bullet racing past his shoulder.

I've got to do something, he thought. The words of his old college professor flashed through his mind: *The best defense is a good offense.* When Ben dropped out of sight momentarily on the back of the hill he veered sharply to his right, ran for five yards, and dropped to the ground, gasping for breath. In a minute he crawled back to the ridge of the hill, and was shocked to see just how close his pursuers were. Lying on his stomach, with his arms stretched out in front of him, holding the Weasel's pistol with both hands, he fired at the lead man. For a moment he thought he had missed, but then saw the man fall forward face down without losing any of his momentum, plowing up the dirt in front of him before finally coming to a stop in a cloud of dust.

The man running behind him tripped over the body and with a scream fell into a prickly pear cactus. The others ground to a halt, trying to determine what had happened. Ben fired again, and another of the pursuers fell to the ground, yelling in pain. The rest of the men quickly ducked for cover.

THE THIRD MUSKETEER

For a few moments there was complete silence except for the cries and curses of the man covered with cactus needles. Gradually the chatter began to pick up from the men, but it was all in Spanish so Ben couldn't tell what they were saying. Once again Ben became aware of a throbbing pain in his shoulder. Crashing into the Weasel hadn't helped any, but it didn't look like the wound had been reopened.

Ben decided to send another shot into the rocks below just to let them know he was still around, but the pistol clicked on empty. He discarded the gun and pulled Beefy's revolver from his belt. He shot at a shadow he saw moving in the brush, and was rewarded with another outburst of oaths in Spanish.

Through the moonlight Ben thought he saw movement both to the right and to the left of where the men had ducked for cover. *Makes sense*, he thought. *They will try a pincher movement and come at me from the sides.*

Ben crawled back down the hill and took off running 50 yards further, before once again dropping to the ground while still trying to catch his breath. It wasn't long before he saw two hombres cautiously approach his previous position, one coming in from one side and one from the other. When they realized he was not there, they shouted back to their comrades who came up slowly, nervously looking to their right and left.

"Amigos," Ben shouted. "Your benefactors are all dead. You no longer work for them. Your position with Senior Sanchez is over. So you now have no quarrel with me. Why would you die for no reason? The Federals will be here soon. I have called them. If I were you, I would not want to be around when they find the bodies. You will not be sent back to Mexico, you will go to prison for the rest of your lives. You should leave while you still have the chance."

Ben watched them as they huddled together and engaged in animated discussion. Then one turned and yelled back. "Senior, you are right. We leave you now. Go in peace."

Ben saw the men turn and return the way they had come. *I don't think they'll bother me anymore*, he thought, *but I'm not going to press my luck.*

He remembered that after leaving Taos they had made only two turns, both to the left. That would mean they had turned once to the west, and then to the south. They had been on a smooth highway for all but the last mile or so. He figured from all of this that they must have turned west onto Highway 64 out of Taos, and that the ranch must be several miles south of that road. He could see the Sangre De Cristo Mountains in the distance, illuminated by the bright moonlight. He knew this would be to his east. He decided to head north, hoping to reach the highway leading back to Taos.

After walking at a fast clip for 20 minutes, he stopped and lay down on top of a small hill to rest and to see if his pursuers were still following. He heard nothing. Ten minutes later he decided that they had given up the chase, not willing to run into another ambush with a man with a gun. Ben surmised that these men were some of the same ones that had attacked Brady and himself in Colorado. Probably illegals. But by now they must have realized that Ben was not important to them with their employer dead, and that the best thing for them was to get back to the ranch and pack up their things before the police arrived.

Ben walked for 30 minutes before intersecting the highway. He followed it to the right, heading for the mountains dimly visible in the east. There was almost no traffic, but when a car or truck came by Ben hid at the side of the road. He didn't want to be caught in the open by any of Sanchez's men. Even though they were probably now on the run, they might still like revenge on the man responsible for it all if given an opportunity.

As the sky began to lighten in the east Ben saw the bridge that crosses the Rio Grande River come into view. He knew this was just about ten miles north of Taos. When he came to the rim of the canyon he was struck once again with the rugged beauty of the gorge. Over the centuries the river had worn a chasm 650 feet deep and 1,000 feet across. The sides were almost perpendicular, impossible to cross even on foot. Ben had read somewhere that the bridge over the narrow canyon was the third highest in the United States, and was a national historical site.

There was a parking and picnic area on the west side of the ravine and even though it was early in the morning several cars were there now as tourists parked and walked out over the overpass to gaze at the stream meandering far below. Some of the vacationers were enjoying hot coffee at the picnic tables. Ben approached an elderly couple to see if he could beg a ride from them, but when they saw him coming they quickly turned their backs and pointedly stared the other way. Looking down at his shirt, Ben realized how disreputable he appeared. His shirt was dirty and stained with blood, and there was a tear in the leg of his pants. He didn't remember when that had happened. He imagined his face didn't look much different than his clothes.

Ben spotted a rest room in the camp area and ducked in. Fortunately it had running water so he was able to wash his face and freshen up a bit, although he didn't have a comb to run through his unruly hair.

When he came out he saw three young men coming back from the bridge. *Look like college kids*, Ben thought. He approached them, explained that his rental car had broken down, and that he'd had a rough night walking along the road to get here. He offered them $10 for a ride into Taos where he could contact the rental agency. They readily accepted. On the way, Ben learned they were going to Albuquerque, so offered them $100 if they would take him to Old Town in the city.

They left him in the plaza and he walked over to the parking area where he had left his rental car. It was still there. He retrieved his cell phone from the glove compartment and called Suzie.

"Hi, Suzie. This is Ben. I've got good news and bad news," he said. There was a moment's pause before she answered.

"Ben! Where are you? What's happened?" she demanded.

"Well, the good news is that Sanchez is definitely the man we saw leaving Sawyer's house in Oldvil. The bad news is that I had to kill him."

Another moment of shocked silence. "All right Mr. Ben Foxworth. I've got my breath back. Now how about telling me just where you are and what is going on. From the beginning!"

So Ben related his experiences over the past day and a half. "I'm afraid I left somewhat of a mess at the ranch. My guess is that Sanchez had some kind of smuggling operation going on across the border. People and drugs coming this way. Probably guns going south. I'm guessing some of the illegals he brought across were criminals, and he hired them into his organization. All of this is pure conjecture, of course. But I would bet that this is where the men came from that attacked Brady and me in Colorado. I would guess that the ranch has been abandoned by now and is pretty much the way I left it with bodies in the house and out on the desert. Those guys wouldn't want to be hanging around after their little operation has blown wide open."

"Did Sanchez say anything?" Suzie asked. "Anything at all that would indicate who the other terrorist might be or what their plans were?"

"Nothing at all. Except that he was the one that killed Buddy and the other agent in Oldville. It wasn't Gene after all. He didn't say anything about killing John though. Or trying to kill me. That must have been someone else."

"You're probably right," Suzie said. "As I said before it's my guess that all three of them were there for a meeting, and when Sanchez discovered that Sawyer's house was being watched, and he had been seen, he decided to eliminate the two agents, and make sure they had no photos. In all likelihood, it was left to the third terrorist to take care of you and John the next night while he silenced Sawyer."

"I really have a rough time seeing Sanchez as a terrorist. As a cheap, opportunistic thug who is out for whatever he can get—yes. But as an idealistic Muslim terrorist? He just doesn't fit the picture."

"You never can tell," Suzie replied. "These guys have been trained to assume roles that completely disguise their true identities. If he looked the part of a terrorist he wouldn't be any good. Now tell me again how to find this ranch. I'll see that everything is taken care of by the boys at our Albuquerque office."

"By the way," she added, "I guess you are a free man now. Your threat to Sanchez is over. Are you headed back to your home?"

"I am. How is Brady doing?"

"He's just fine. Giving the hospital nurses a fit as I understand with his Irish brogue. He should be released any day now. I'm headed to Albuquerque just as fast as I can. When things are wrapped up there, I'll swing up to Colorado. I'd like to talk with you some more about everything you found out from Sanchez."

"Unfortunately, it was very little."

Checking his cell phone Ben noted that his daughter had called three times. With a sigh he dialed her number. Maybe she was right. Maybe he was getting too old for all of this excitement and needed to sell his place and move into an old fogey's retirement community where things were much calmer and more predictable. Right now that sounded pretty good.

Ben returned to his motel after assuring his daughter that he was OK. He debated between taking a shower first or crashing in the bed. The bed won out.

CHAPTER TWELVE

The flame seared the five rib eye steaks as the juices dripped onto the hot coals, sending a few sparks rising into the cool mountain air. Ben felt the meat with the tip of his spatula, and decided they were just about done—medium rare as ordered.

Just then the door to the kitchen of his house opened and Ann stuck her head out. "How are they coming, oh mighty chef?" she asked.

Ben looked up and thought once again how attractive Ann was, even in her 60's. She had changed her hair style from Oldvil. Instead of being tightly combed back, which had given her a somewhat severe look, it now flowed freely, framing her face with a soft reddish glow.

Ben was suddenly overtaken with a similar picture from the distant past. It was the week of their high school graduation. Ben's Mom had invited Ben's friends over for a party, and since his Dad was away on business, Ben had been barbequing the hamburgers on a grill on their back porch. He remembered Ann sticking her head out of the kitchen door, exactly as she was doing now, asking how the hamburgers were coming.

"I think they're done," he replied now as he had back then. *Funny how life seems to come full circle*, he thought, as he lifted the steaks onto the platter. Inside the kitchen Ann was getting the potatoes out of the oven while Brady was putting the finishing touches on his special "Isle of the Green" salad, using spices and other ingredients known only to him.

On the other end of the porch Suzie and Donald Klein were in deep conversation. Suzie pointed to Ben, obviously making some kind of point about his recent escapades. Again Ben was overcome by a feeling that all of this had happened before. *I must be getting old*, he thought. *Everything seems like it's the second time around. Maybe it all happened in some other lifetime. As the man says, déjà vu all over again.*

Brady had been released from the hospital the day before, and accepted Ben's offer to recuperate at his place. All of the damages to the house from the attack the previous week had been repaired, except, if one happened to notice, for two bullet holes in the ceiling. Suzie had flown in from Albuquerque after supervising the clean-up at Sanchez's ranch.

The police report given to the press said that Sanchez had been killed by illegal immigrants staying at his ranch. The people of New Mexico were shocked to discover that Sanchez had been running a smuggling operation, dealing with people, guns and drugs. A large supply of marijuana was discovered at the ranch. No mention was made of any terrorist activities on the part of the man running for the Senate however, nor any hint that he might be a Muslim terrorist. And absolutely nothing about Ben.

Sara, Brady's fiancée, was visiting for a few days. She had been beside herself when Brady was shot, and had flown into the Springs the same day that Ben had left for New York. She only stayed for one day then, but was now back for a week's vacation.

Ben invited Ann for the weekend, and as an after thought extended the invitation to Donald Klein. Ben wasn't too keen about the idea, but didn't like the thought of Ann driving down from Denver by herself. Ben had three guest rooms; Ann and Sara were sharing one, Suzie was in another and Donald had the third. Brady opted to move to the couch.

Ann, as well as Ben, had taken an immediate liking to Sara. She was small with a great figure. Light ebony skin that exhibited warmth and vitality and a turned up petite nose. But it was her eyes that revealed the loving and compassionate woman inside. *I can see why she would be such a great doctor*, Ben thought upon meeting her. She was a person you would immediately want to take into your confidence.

She and Ben had talked about her work one afternoon when Brady was off jogging.

"I know my being a doctor bothers Brady," she said. "His idea of a wife is someone who stays at home and mends his socks. Not that that isn't important," she added hastily, remembering that Ben's wife had not worked. "But for me I have somewhat different goals and different ambitions. I want to help people. It's what I'm good at, and what I enjoy. Brady wouldn't like me nearly as much if I weren't who I was meant to be."

"He'll come around," Ben assured her. "He loves you, and deep down is very proud of who you are. I know he wouldn't dream of asking you to give up something that is so important to you."

"I realize that," she said, "but is he willing to live with it? Can we really have a happy marriage?"

"Your marriage will be whatever the two of you want it to be. And I have no doubt that you can both pursue your careers and maintain a very stable and wonderful home life for your family."

"Oh I hope so. I do love the galoot in spite of his old fashioned views on a woman's place in the world."

As they gathered for dinner Brady rose to propose a toast.

"I bet it's one of your Irish grandfather's old sayings," Ben interjected.

"Aye, and a grand old man he was. And how often I remember him laying this very blessing on me that I am about to pass on to all of you." Ignoring everyone's collective groan, he raised his glass of wine on high.

"May each of you have warm words on a cold evening, a full moon on a dark night, and the road downhill all the way to your door."

"Hear, hear," everyone responded.

Brady ducked as Sara threw a wadded napkin at him.

After supper the group moved to the back porch for a second cup of coffee. The night was getting chilly, but Ben had a large fire going in the outside fireplace.

"All right," Ann said, "I've held my curiosity long enough. Who's going to tell me exactly what happened? I know that Brady here is recovering from a gun wound, and apparently Ben is no longer considered to be in any danger. Have you caught the bad guys?"

"Well, I guess a good place to start would be for Brady and me to compare our wounds to see who got shot up the worst," Ben said, and made as if to pull up his shirt.

"I think we can do without that," Ann hastily replied. "Not that we girls wouldn't mind gazing at some male abs, but the issue here is—is it all over?"

Ben looked to Suzie, who looked to Brady, who looked to Ben.

"Well then, 'tis like this," Brady finally responded. "Our trouble-making friend here—Mr. Benjamin Foxworth himself—

decided he would attempt to solve this case with only minimal help from the likes of us FBI types. As you might already know, the bad guys tried to put the finger on Ben again right here in this very garden spot, but he was able to scare them off, with a little help from yours truly, I might add. But in the process a stray bullet took a liking to my shoulder. So while I was attending to this minor distraction, Ben took off for the citadel in the East. He went to Bamford Law School—that prestigious institution that your esteemed classmate, Gene Sawyer attended, and fortuitously discovered a picture in an old year book that looked suspiciously like the mystery gentleman that the three of them saw leaving Sawyer's house back in Oldvil. Now this is not for public knowledge, but it turns out our man was none other than Mr. Anthony Sanchez, popular politician from New Mexico, who was running for the Senate. Perhaps the hero of the hour will tell us what happened next in his very own words," Brady said.

Ben suspected Suzie and Brady wanted to see if he had the story down pat.

"Not much more to tell," Ben said. "I found a picture that looked like our man, but of course it was taken quite some years ago. From the internet I found that he was living in Albuquerque, running for the Senate, so decided that I should try to see him in the flesh to determine if he was indeed our Mr. X. That's why I was there when we all got together last week. Turns out he was the man, so I notified Suzie here, but before anyone could move in he was unfortunately killed by some illegal immigrants staying at his ranch. Seems that in addition to everything else he had a smuggling operation going, and apparently something back fired on him. Strange twist of events."

"But as I recall," Ann said, "there were three Islamic terrorists planning something awful. What were their names—Al Kabi or something and Mullah and somebody else. Which one was Sanchez, and do you know who the third one is, or what it is they are planning?"

"I guess the answer is "no" to both questions," Suzie replied. We think Gene Sawyer was Al Kahfi. Kahfi, by the way, not Kabi. The other two, based on the intel we have, are Fatim and Mullah. But we don't know which one Sanchez was. Nor do we have any clue as to the terrorist act they were—or maybe still are—planning. They apparently kept no written records or notes, nothing on any computers, or anything that we could find. We suspect that Sanchez, however, is the one with the kind of connections that could provide them with the explosives they used at the memorials in Washington. And it just so happens that he was in Washington when the attacks occurred."

"So this terrorist was almost elected to our Senate. That is scary," Donald said.

"But remember, this is just between us for now," Suzie replied. "We felt it would be best to keep this aspect of his life quiet for the moment so as not to unduly alert the third member of their cell."

"So there's still one terrorist out there. And as far as we know, still planning some terrible attack against us?" Ann said.

"I'm afraid that's about it," Suzie replied.

"Maybe he'll do us all a favor and blow up Hollywood," Donald said. "That certainly would not be a loss."

They all chuckled at the thought.

"If I were a guessing man," Ben said, "I'd bet that the next target is going to be a religious one. I can't get over the look in Sawyer's eyes when he said that if you can kill religion in a nation, you can kill the nation."

"In that case," Ann said, "you should definitely look into the ACLU. I think they are dedicated to killing religion for all of us."

"Well then," Brady said, "that's a pretty serious charge to be making against an organization dedicated to preserving our very liberties. All they want to do is to keep religion out of the public square."

"Just like smoking," Ben joined in. "We have banned smoking in all public places. What kind of message does that send to our youth?"

"Hopefully that smoking is bad for you and is not an accepted form of behavior in our society," Brady replied.

"Exactly. So when we also ban religion from all public places, doesn't that send the same message to our youth? That being religious is an unacceptable form of social behavior? Or at least that it should be practiced only in the privacy of your home and church? That it is offensive to the mainstream of our culture?"

Donald cleared his throat. "I might say, this conversation leads to a very strange and troubling set of coincidences. As Ann knows, a large Christian conference is being planned in Denver for next month. Leaders of all major denominations are coming together to discuss common problems facing our faith. I have been put in charge of handling the physical arrangements, something I have had considerable experience with at our college, although on a much smaller scale, and because I live in the vicinity. One of the guest speakers is Norman Stepps, head of the California ACLU. He has been invited to clarify the ACLU's stand on religion and government."

"And another speaker," Suzie interjected in a soft voice, "is— or was to have been—our very own Anthony Sanchez. I saw that on his calendar."

"Exactly," Donald continued. "He was to speak to us about the problem with illegal immigration."

"So here you have the head of the ACLU in California and Sanchez coming together at the largest Christian conference we have ever seen," Ben mused. "And by my way of thinking both of them are terrorists, although in different ways. And we believe terrorists are planning some kind of attack on the Christian community, and that it is scheduled to be any day now."

The group fell silent as they digested this bit of news.

"Never did believe in coincidences," Ben said. "I sure would like to have 10 minutes with this Stepps fellow. Just to see what kind of guy he is."

Donald looked a little uncomfortable as he squirmed in his chair. "It just so happens that I am meeting with Mr. Stepps in Denver next week. He is here on other business, and wanted to check out the facilities at the convention center and to discus the presentation aids he would need for his talk."

"'Check out the facilities at the convention center,'" Ann said. "That sounds ominous."

"Donald, old buddy, how about letting me sit in on that meeting?" Ben said.

"Now just a minute," Suzie interjected. "Ben, you have mingled with FBI business too much already. Not that we don't appreciate what you've done, but you just stay out of this. If anyone sits in on that meeting it will be Brady and myself."

"Might I say that this seems just a wee bit looney-toonie," Brady said. "Suzie, we don't have one shred of evidence that would implicate our Mr. Stepps in anything. Not one iota! Nothing but some very wild speculation. We might just as well be accusing the wee fairies in good old Ireland based on what we know."

"Brady is right," Ben said. "This is about as far out as you can get. It would be counterproductive to involve the FBI at this time. We wouldn't want to alert Stepps to the fact that he was a suspect, if that's what we considered him. But I could sit in on the meeting as a lawyer for the conference, you know, just checking to make sure nothing was said or done that might have any legal ramifications for the Christian council. And I could goad him a little to see how he reacts. As a lawyer I've had a lot of experience reading peoples' character under duress."

"Hold on there," Donald said. "I don't have any authority to have you or anybody else in my meeting with Stepps. This is strictly church business. I can't have you coming in like a bull in a china closet putting him through a third degree."

"Ben is probably right," Suzie said. "And Donald, all we are trying to do here is to look out for the conference's safety. If you are in charge of facilities, this should certainly come under your area of responsibility. Of course, we could always put some official pressure on the council if that's what you need, but I think it would be far preferable to keep this just among ourselves. Most likely we are completely off base here anyway."

"My old law professor used to say that if you really wanted to know about a man's character, you need to get him good and angry," Ben mused.

"I don't like this," Donald said. "Don't like it at all."

CHAPTER THIRTEEN

The Colorado Convention Center is a gigantic two-story building located in the heart of the city, providing 584,000 square feet of meeting rooms, exhibit halls, ballrooms and a 5,000 seat theater known as the Wells Fargo Theater. It promised to be an excellent setting for the Christian Coalition assembly.

In one of the smaller meeting rooms Ben, Donald and Norman Stepps sat around a table, winding up a tour of the facility given by one of the staff members. They had looked in on numerous meetings currently underway—the National Fly Fishing Association, the Art Institute of Colorado, the Denver Public School System and the National Association of Heath Care Providers.

"The facilities here are wonderful," Stepps was saying. "Probably the best I have ever seen. It will be an honor to speak to your group in such a setting." Norman Stepps was a tall, willowy man, who looked like he hadn't had a good meal in weeks. His face was long and narrow, with thin grey hair coming down over his forehead, parted in the middle. His eyes were pin points of blue, and had a steady, searching look. He was wearing a white seersucker suit which was highlighted by a bright purple tie.

"I'm glad you find them satisfactory," Donald replied. "We anticipate having standing room only in the Wells Fargo Theater for your presentation. Is there anything else you will need?"

"No, I think not."

Ben had been silent through most of the tour, but now spoke up. "Mr. Stepps, I have just a couple of questions for you, as the legal counsel for the group. Do you plan to aim your comments at a general level, or will you get into specific cases in which the ACLU is involved?"

"I haven't really finalized my thoughts on the presentation. Did you have something in mind?"

Donald shifted uneasily in his seat and gave Ben a despairing look, but kept silent.

"Well, for instance the law suit the ACLU has brought against the state of Kentucky challenging their attempt to restrict demonstrations at funerals of military personnel. I know this is somewhat out of your district, but are you familiar with the case?"

Stepps smiled broadly and straightened in his chair. "Yes, sir. I am." He was obviously eager for the questions he knew would be coming.

Ben continued, "Apparently this group, the Salvation Unified Church out of Peoria, Wisconsin, believes that God is punishing America for condoning homosexuals. And He is doing this by letting our soldiers be killed in combat, and according to them it is entirely fitting that these servicemen die. Church members have gone all over the country to disrupt military funerals by mocking these deaths."

Ben referred to a paper he held in his hand. "Some of the banners they carry and slogans they shout at these demonstrations include such things as 'God Hates Fags,' 'Thank God for Roadside Bombs,' 'Thank God for Dead Soldiers' and

'Don't Worship the Dead.' Would you not agree, Mr. Stepps, that these actions are disgraceful and infringe on the rights of a grieving family who are in the process of burying their loved one? Should these families not be able to do so in privacy and with dignity without being harassed by some fringe religious group?"

"As despicable as I may find these actions personally, I must state that these protesters are entirely within their rights to express their views. We cannot prohibit freedom of speech or put time limits on it, even if we find it repulsive. We at the ACLU will vigorously defend this group's right to state their opinions."

"So you are saying," Ben observed, "that everyone has an absolute right to express their views in a public place, even though they may be religious in nature and even though they may be offensive to some."

"That is correct—as long as they are on public land and not transgressing on private property. And a cemetery is normally open to the public." Stepps leaned back in his chair with a smug look on his face, obviously feeling that he had clearly made his point.

"And I believe the ACLU has said there can be no time restraint placed on the demonstration?"

"That is correct. You cannot put any limits on an individual's right of speech."

"So they could demonstrate all afternoon—or all day—or all year for that matter. Even forever if they were so inclined?"

"That is somewhat ridiculous, but yes they could demonstrate till the end of time if they chose."

"Then why is it that in San Diego the ACLU has been fighting for years against the right of the citizens of that fair city to display a cross on a war memorial on top of Mount

Soldad? These are citizens expressing their faith in God in a public location. Are they not entitled to the same rights as the radical religious group you are defending?"

Stepps paused and gave Ben a harsh look as he suddenly realized the trap Ben had led him into. But he raised his head and replied, somewhat defiantly, "I think we are talking about two entirely different situations here. A group of protesters carrying placards is not the same thing as the government erecting a permanent memorial cast in stone on public lands supporting one religion over all others."

"First of all," Ben replied, "the government didn't erect the cross. It was paid for through private donations. And the citizens of San Diego recently voted overwhelming in support of the monument. Let me restate what you agreed with only moments ago. A group has an absolute right to express their views in a public place, whether it is religious in nature or regardless if some may feel offended by it. And there can be no time restraint placed on them—it can be for a day or forever. Why does this not pertain to the Mt. Soldad case you are so ardently prosecuting?"

"Just what is your agenda here, Mr. Foxworth? It obviously has nothing to do with the convention."

Ben glared at Stepps, then in a harsh, accusatory tone, said, "My agenda, as you call it, is to satisfy my belief that you are totally inconsistent in your application of the law, but completely consistent in your persecution of Christianity." These were jarring words intended to push Stepps to the brink, but he merely gave Ben a thin, humorless smile and said nothing more. Ben's attempt to goad the man into some intemperate remark was not working.

At this point Donald put a restraining hand on Ben's arm and gave him an exasperated look. "Please accept my apologies, Mr. Stepps," he said. "I'm afraid my colleague here has gotten rather far afield. Let me assure you that there will be no such repetition at the conference. I think we have said quite enough for this meeting. I sincerely regret any differences in opinion that might have been expressed here. I do thank you for coming and for your patience."

"I do not object to legitimate questions," Stepps said, "but Mr. Foxworth has misconstrued my words to meet his own view of the world. The ACLU will adamantly protest any infringement on the principal of separation of church and state, but at the same time will strenuously support every group's right to freedom of expression. I think that pretty much sums up our position in these matters."

Donald hurried over to Stepps, shaking his hand and patting him on the back, talking all the while, trying to mitigate the offensiveness of Ben's attack. Ben watched carefully as the tall and lean lawyer rose from his chair, talked briefly with Donald, and then gathered up his papers. He gave Ben a withering scowl as he turned and walked to the door.

Later Ben and Donald met with Suzie and Brady, who had been following their tour from a distance.

"I have never been so embarrassed," Donald said. "Ben was not only impolite, he actually bullied the man. I hope word of this doesn't get back to the conference planners."

Brady gave Donald a sympathetic look, and then winked at Ben. "Well, did you wring anything out of our suspect to confirm our very wild speculations?" he asked.

"Nothing at all, I'm afraid," Ben said. "I wish I had pressed him on the ACLU's failure to object to some of the Muslim religious demands on our schools and universities. Like having the schools set aside a time and room for their prayers, and facilities for them to wash their feet. It would have been interesting to see if he objected to this as strongly as he does when

Christians want to start the day with prayer." Ben shook his head. "I guess I don't know what to think. I don't like the guy, and he's a pretty cool customer when under duress. Still, I must admit I have a hard time seeing him as a terrorist. Of course, I have a hard time picturing Gene Sawyer as a terrorist too. At any rate I would say that we should keep a very close watch on our Mr. Stepps at the conference. Maybe this is a long shot, based on nothing at all, but I wouldn't want to gamble anyone's life on it."

"I agree," Suzie said. "We ran a background check on him, but didn't come up with anything significant. He grew up in a small town in Montana where his Dad was a high school teacher. Got his college degree and law degree from Cal at Berkley."

"That figures," Ben said.

"He got a job in the District Attorney's office in Missoula after graduation," Brady said. "Worked there several years before being hired by the ACLU. Made frequent trips back east in connection with his job, including several to New York, but we can't tie him to Bamford Law School or our Muslim mosque. Two years ago he was in Albuquerque at a work shop on civil rights, but again no way of knowing whether he could have been in contact with Sanchez or not."

"Nevertheless," Suzie said, "I think it is entirely likely that this conference might be the target that our terrorists have in their sight. It just seems like too good of an opportunity to let slip by. We know that Sawyer seemed to indicate that the next attack might be against organized religion, and that at least one of our terrorists was going to be here for this conference. I'm going to convince my boss to let Brady and me cover security for the event. That way we can be here and keep an eye open for anything out of the ordinary. And we can keep our Mr. Stepps under close observation."

They left the building with Donald still mumbling about the harsh treatment of his guest.

CHAPTER FOURTEEN

Two weeks later the Convention Center was a beehive of activity with over 4,000 delegates gathered for the conference. The lobbies were surging with people—pastors, priests, lay persons, reporters, salespeople and uniformed security staff. The second floor exhibit hall was filled with displays of church furniture—pews, tables, pulpits—clerical robes, literature, religious memorabilia, pianos, organs, sound systems, Sunday School lesson material, jewelry, clothing and of course bumper stickers.

Security was tight, supervised by Suzie and Brady. Suzie had demanded floor plans of the entire building, and had studied them carefully to make sure she knew every inch of the structure. Much to the dismay of the conference staff she had insisted that the public only be allowed to gain entrance to the hall through the doors on 14th Street, and everyone had to pass through metal detectors.

The opening day went without a hitch, and everyone heaved a sigh of relief. But they knew that there were three more days to go, and Stepps wasn't due to arrive until the second day.

The next morning Suzie and Brady held a 7:00 meeting with the entire security staff to review the previous day's successes and failures. Brady felt some of the screeners had been a little lax during the afternoon hours, and wanted to make sure they remained vigilant throughout the day.

Later in the morning Ben was standing on the stairs in the front lobby, searching the sea of bodies surging and milling below for any sign of Suzie. Ben had encountered no trouble in getting a pass for the convention from Donald.

Both Suzie and Brady had disappeared shortly after the early morning meeting, and it was now almost 10:00. As he looked out over the mass of bodies swirling in the lobby in every direction, he saw Anthony Stepps arrive at the entrance. After passing through the electronic screening he was pulled to one side where he was manually patted down for any concealed objects. The guard explained that they were doing more extensive searches on random participants, and Stepps just happened to be the next one. Stepps obviously wasn't buying that story, knowing that he had been singled out because he was with the ACLU.

After clearing the security station, Stepps looked back to the entrance of the building as if he might be looking for someone. *He knows he was being followed*, Ben thought. *Or at least suspects that he was. Wonder if he detected his tail? Doesn't matter, he'll have two new ones here.*

Ben spotted them in the crowd. One was a woman, Martha was her name, who was chatting animatedly with a group of conventioneers. The other, Jacob, was idly reading a program while holding a paper cup of coffee. Both had one eye on Stepps, and were ready to move out as soon as he did.

Stepps surveyed the crowd in the lobby, and spotted Ben standing on the stairs. His stern expression gave way to a sardonic grin, and he nodded slightly in a greeting. Ben smiled, and raised his hand in a return gesture. Stepps turned and proceeded down the hall to the theater. The two FBI agents were close behind.

Just then he heard his name being called from below, and spotted April Showers—Means—and Henry just below him at the foot of the stairs.

"Ben Foxworth," April was saying, "now aren't you a sight for these old eyes. I must say, you're looking much better than last time I saw you in Oldvil."

"Hi April, Henry." Ben came down the stairs and shook their hands. "Ann told me you two were attending the shindig here. You're staying with her while you're in Denver?"

"Yup. We're here until Thursday," Henry replied. "April was selected as a delegate from our Presbytery, and I'm just tagging along to make sure she doesn't run off with some other fellow." Henry looked different than he did back in their kitchen in Oldville with his large body stuffed into a suit that looked two sizes too small, his hair slicked down and sporting a bright red tie.

As they were talking, Ben saw Suzie arrive at the front entrance, carrying a small satchel. She flashed her badge to the door guards and walked around the metal detectors. *Bet she's packing some hardware that would set those detectors singing*, Ben thought.

"Hey, guys," Ben said, "I've got to run. I'll probably see you at Ann's sometime this week. Be sure to take notes on the ACLU presentation," and he rushed off.

For a moment Ben lost sight of Suzie in the throng of people, but then spotted her heading down the main hallway to the rear of the center. Ben hurried after her, struggling to get through the mass of bodies in the lobby. He reached the hallway just in time to see her going into a maintenance area at the rear of the building. By time Ben got there, she had disappeared, but Ben saw that the service elevator was stopping at the custodian floor at the top of the building, which was strictly a working area for the center's intricate system of air conditioning vents.

Ben punched the elevator button and waited impatiently for it to return to the main level. Finally he realized that the elevator was not moving. *I bet she blocked it to keep it up there,* Ben thought, and hurried off to find the stairs that would lead to the upper level. When at last he found them he bounded up the steps two at a time and rushed into the top floor which housed a labyrinth of ducts carrying air conditioning to the entire building. He strode through the maze looking for any sign of Suzie. He heard a soft pop and a louder bang near the back of the area, and finally spotted her standing beside one of the huge air ducts. Her open briefcase was lying by her side, and she was holding a large empty tube in her hand. On the floor at her feet lay a battery-operated drill.

"Suzie, what are you doing?" he asked.

She whirled around at the sound of his voice, at the same time pulling a Smith and Wesson M&P service revolver from her briefcase.

"Hello, Ben. I'm afraid I've got bad news for you," she said, with a crooked smile on her face. "Your hypocritical Christians below us are getting a good dose of anthrax as we speak. As you may know this particular duct goes to the Wells Fargo Theater, where there are probably 4,000 people right now eager to listen to your Mr. Stepps. I have just released 1 kilogram of anthrax, enough to kill at least half of those below."

"But Suzie—you? How could you do this?"

"Pretty simple really. I just drilled a hole into the duct, held the container you see at my feet against the hole, and the air sucked the entire contents of anthrax into the duct. It is being blown throughout the theater right now and there is nothing you can do about it."

"But—I don't understand. You're telling me that you are a terrorist? Why, for God's sake?"

"I am a reformer, Ben. Someone who will help save this country from the decadence and debauchery it has fallen into. Islam will be the salvation of all mankind. It will replace the immorality that has overrun us. Greed, lies, rape, homosexuality, dishonesty in all levels of government. All that is going to change, Ben, and I will have helped make it possible."

"I learned long ago that our laws only protect the privileged," she continued. "I discovered that fact of life when I was only thirteen, and continually violated by my own father and the law would do nothing about it. Don't talk to me about justice under this government. Everyone is corrupt from the top down. And by the way, you can call me by the name I prefer, Fatima Rashid. You know me as Fatim, a man's name, but Fatima is the female form of the word. We felt it would be more impressive shortening it to the male version."

"So is this the major attack we have been looking for," Ben asked. "Somehow it seems more like a target of opportunity than something being planned months ago."

"No, this conference has been our objective from the very start, but we weren't quite sure how we were going to work it. You helped us out there, with your suspicions of the ACLU. Gave me a chance to convince my superiors that Brady and I needed to be assigned to the meeting to oversee security. But I'm afraid this conversation is at an end, Ben. Probably you've already been exposed to a lethal dose of anthrax, unless you've been immunized against it as I have, but I'm in kind of a hurry, you see. I've got a plane to catch for Mexico."

Suzie raised the pistol, took aim at Ben's chest, and pulled the trigger. Ben's heart almost stopped, but nothing happened. No pop from the gun, no repercussion, and most importantly, no bullet firing. Suzie looked at the pistol in surprise, then took aim once again and squeezed the trigger. Again nothing happened.

"I'm afraid they're blanks," Brady said, as he stepped from behind a column in back of Ben, with his Beretta 9mm drawn and pointing towards Suzie. "Must be a wee bit disappointing, I'm sure. But I took the liberty of replacing all of your bullets last evening while you were at dinner with shells that have no powder."

"Man, you took your time," Ben said to Brady. "At the last minute there I wasn't sure you were anywhere around."

"I was right behind you, old buddy. Just wanted to give my partner here time to incriminate herself beyond any doubt. You do have your pocket recorder turned on, don't you?"

"It's on," Ben said. "But I would have thought being caught red-handed would have been evidence enough."

"You can never be bloody certain. Being an officer of the law she could have made up any number of plausible reasons why she was here when she was. Enough maybe for a reasonable doubt. But now there will be no question."

"You may have me," Suzie snarled, "but you can't save your precious congregation below. They've already been exposed."

"Exposed to a strain of anthrax which is used in animal vaccination programs," Brady replied, "which is not a significant risk to humans. It's a long story, you see, but I know you stole the anthrax from that FBI training center we both attended. They liked to impress the trainees by telling them that the container on display contained enough anthrax to kill 4,000 people. Anthrax sealed tightly in a container within a container and in a locked room. This was true as far as it went. But the capsule on display contained a strain of anthrax used in animal vaccinations which is harmless to humans. 'Twas not the Ames anthrax—the aerosol deadly strain—which sure enough could kill thousands. And 'tis that very capsule that I see now at your feet. Did you not wonder why there was no more publicity than there was when it was stolen? Didn't want to create a panic, they told everyone. But they weren't all that worried, because they knew it wasn't harmful to humans. I learned all this from a friend who worked there. I confirmed that this was what you had in your room when I changed the bullets for your gun. So you see, dear lady, all of your hard work and masterful deception is for naught."

While Brady was talking, Suzie's right hand had shifted to her right hip, and was slowly moving behind her back. Too late Ben realized she was pulling a small 2 inch revolver from a belt in her back. Ben recognized it as a Rossi .38 caliber sub-compact, a gun not much bigger than a person's hand.

"Look out, Brady!" he shouted. "She's got another gun."

Suzie and Brady both fired at the same time. Both hit their target. Brady staggered and fell on his back, dropping his gun to the floor. Suzie also fell to her knees, but didn't lose consciousness. She raised her hand gun again, and fired at Ben. This time her mark was wild, the bullet plunging into the duct work behind him. Ben dove for the floor, grabbing Brady's gun as he fell. With one swift, fluid movement he grasped the gun with both hands and fired two shots at Suzie's sagging body. She fell back without a sound.

* * * * *

Once again Brady, Donald and Ann were gathered at Ben's home for a barbequed steak dinner. The weather was considerably cooler than on the previous cook-out, so everyone but Ben stayed inside while he braved the elements and fired up the pit. Later they had a small glass of Bailey's in front of the fireplace while Ben put on a disc of Sinatra melodies.

"I still can't believe Suzie was actually a terrorist," Ann said. "Somehow she just didn't look the part."

"She was a pretty bitter woman," Brady replied. "Had a miserable childhood. Her Mom died when Suzie was just a wee one, and her Dad abused her for years. She complained to the Children's Welfare Office, but nothing was ever proved and they took no action. She was exposed to Islam at the Kabil Omar mosque in New York years ago. You know, the one near the Bamford Law School. That's where she met up with Sawyer and Sanchez. I guess she saw fundamentalist Islam as the answer to the world's problems. Or at least her problems."

"So when did you begin to suspect that she might be one of the terrorists?" Ann asked.

"I guess it wasn't any one thing in particular," Ben said. "More like a combination of coincidences and impressions that got me to wondering. First of all I couldn't believe that she had been so careless with the photos of Gene Sawyer's law school classmates that she would have left the picture of Sanchez out of the rogue's gallery. That seemed odd and out of character for her. Then, when I went to Albuquerque, I had the distinct impression that Sanchez was expecting me. Not expecting me sometime, but specifically on that day. Suzie was the only one who knew that I would be there. Also he didn't seem at all worried when I told him the FBI knew where I was. He was more concerned at who else I might have talked with."

"But I think the thing that really set me off was at the barbeque here a few weeks ago. There was a moment on the back deck when I was cooking the steaks that I saw my attacker in Oldvil all over again. Suzie was pointing at me while she was talking with Donald. That sent chills down my spine, because it was the same exact image I have of the person who shot at me at the motel. Same stance, same hunch to the shoulders, same size, same way her feet were spread. *Déjà vu* all over again. That's when I went to Brady and discussed some of these things with him. Turns out he had some suspicions himself—things she had said, unexplained absences when bad things were happening, attitude towards people. Not suspicions of her as a terrorist, but just some things that seemed odd. But after we compared notes, we decided to watch her closely and see if we could come up with any hard evidence to substantiate our wild fantasies."

"Then when yours truly snuck into her room this week when she was at dinner," Brady said, "and discovered the vial of non-lethal anthrax hidden in her suitcase, I knew we were on the right track. But we needed more evidence, so I talked my buddy here, Ben, into wiring himself with the hidden microphone to pick up anything she might say that would be incriminating, and I did the same, hoping one of us could catch her in the act. And by glory we both did."

"Except it would appear that you caught a little more than that with a bullet in your leg," Ann replied.

"Well, as we like to say in dear old Ireland, the best laid plans do oft go astray."

"I thought that was in Scotland," Ben said.

"Whatever. So anyway we know that Sawyer was Al Kahfi, and Suzie was Fatim—or Fatima—so that leaves Sanchez being our Mr. Mullah. Everything wrapped up nice and neat. And even more to the point, my sick leave has been extended two more weeks, and Ben here has promised to make a first class fly fisherman out of me in that time. First test in a couple of days—soon as me leg is a little stronger."

"Assuming you are even able to wade the river with that bum leg of yours," Ben said. "Too badly hurt to go in and sit at a desk, but thinks he can stand all morning in a swift current. Makes you wonder about the tax payer dollars, doesn't it?"

"Ah, but doesn't it give you a sense of security having an officer of the law around giving you protection?" Brady countered.

"Well we hope there's no more need of that," Ann said. "It's such a relief that it's all over."

CHAPTER FIFTEEN

Ben watched the Blue Winged Olive Mayfly drift slowly over the bank of the Platte River, high in the Colorado Rockies, and then descend till it almost touched the clear swift waters, when suddenly it reversed direction and headed back towards the shore and 30 feet beyond. There it changed its course once again and floated back out over the stream. This time Brady allowed the fly to land on the spot he wanted, and he watched intently as the current carried it downstream past a large boulder in the middle of the brook.

I've got to admit, Ben thought, *he's pretty good.*

It was almost impossible to see the dry fly in the swift current, so Ben had tied a strike indicator about five feet up from the fly. This is what Brady kept his eye on as it floated downstream. Brady was almost knee deep in the water at the edge of the river, wearing a pair of hip waders Ben had loaned him. He pulled in the slack line with his left hand as the fly came closer to him, keeping the tip of the fly rod high in the air, and then let it play out as it continued on its course downstream. When nothing happened, Brady pulled in the line and repeated the action, casting the fly far upstream to float past the rock once again. He was positive a large rainbow trout would be swimming in that exact spot.

As he did this, he once again marveled at the beauty of the canyon in which he and Ben were fishing. The river and the dusty road that followed alongside were surrounded by steep rocky cliffs, covered with ponderosa pine and blue spruce. The only sound was the steady murmur of the river and occasionally a crow protesting in the tree tops. It reminded him of one of his favorite spots in Ireland, where he spent much time as a young boy.

Ben, resting on a rock downstream from Brady, decided he had made a good choice in selecting a fly for Brady to use. It resembled the Mayfly dun. As he basked in the sun, which helped to soften the chill of the fall morning, he thought about the life of the Mayfly. It and hundreds of its siblings start their short existence in the rocky bottoms of streams as nymphs, having emerged from eggs laid by their deceased mother. At least once a month in most waters a group of nymphs undergo a transition to a winged insect known as duns. Thousands of duns mature at the same time, floating to the surface and struggling out of their nymphal shucks, drying their wings, and then taking off for new adventures in the bushes and trees along the river. At this stage they have about 24 hours to mate before they die. After mating, the males die and the females return to the water to lay their eggs on the bottom of the stream, after which they also die.

It's when the nymphs start to float to the surface and fight to get out of their shells that trout go on a feeding frenzy. The secret for any fly fisherman is to determine what kind of hatch is occurring at any point in time, since there are literally thousands of species of Mayflies, and then to select a fly that closely resembles the insects.

Ben marveled, as he had many times before, at the complexity and diversity of life existing on this planet. God, or evolution, or more probably both, had certainly created a wondrous universe. But sadly, everything seemed to revolve around a cycle of life and death. *A time for everything*, Ben thought, *just as it says in the Bible.*

"*A time to be born and a time to die…*
A time to keep and a time to throw away…
A time to mourn and a time to dance."

I guess I've been mourning ever since Mary passed away. Maybe it's time I got on with my life. Mary would certainly have wanted me to do that.

Just then Ben saw the strike indicator on Brady's line disappear in the water, indicating that a fish had taken his bait. Brady pulled back on his fly rod, holding the out-going line tight between his finger and the handle to keep the slack from being pulled out by the fish. The fly rod bent almost double as the fish fought against the force that was now restraining it. When the pressure was too strong, Brady released some of the slack and let the trout have its way for a few seconds until it tired, then he gently started pulling the line in once again. When the fish was almost to his body Brady snatched the landing net from his belt and stuck it in the water, trying to bring the rainbow into the mesh. He just about succeeded when the rainbow swam into the rim of the net, which was enough to jar the hook loose. The fish hesitated for a moment until it realized it was free, and then with a swish of its tail disappeared back into the deep waters.

"Too bad," Ben called out. "But you know, you're supposed to bring the fish into the net, not to knock him out with it."

Brady gave Ben a dour look but said nothing as he reeled in the slack line, and then started the process all over again, making dry casts until he had enough line out to place the fly where he wanted.

* * * * *

"Well now, me lad, do I win the first place prize or what?" Brady said at the end of the afternoon. "Five beautiful rainbow, none under seven inches. But I don't know that I like this 'catch and release' idea. They would have made a right tasty dinner for the two of us tonight. As me dear old Irish…"

"Yeah, yeah—I know—your dear old grandfather."

"Exactly. A grand old man he was. He would often comment that a trout in the pan was better than a salmon in the sea."

"And what was that supposed to mean?"

"Something like your bird in the hand being better than one in the bush, I believe. He was partial to salmon any day, but if a trout is what you had, so be it. Anyway, I think I ably demonstrated my fishing skills today."

"Beginners luck," Ben replied. "That's all it was. I watched some of your casts. No skill there."

"Do I detect a bit of jealously, then. And how many did you bring to the net? Three, as I recall."

"I blame it on the cold," Ben said, as he blew warm air onto his hands. "I never do very well when the temperature is at freezing. And it certainly was that today."

Ben and Brady had risen early in the morning and fished the quality waters in Eleven Mile Canyon west of Colorado Springs. The day was clear but chilly. Now they were headed home in Ben's station wagon, with the heater going full blast.

As Ben pulled into the garage, he noticed a note sticking in the front door of the house. After the wagon was unpacked they went inside and Ben retrieved what turned out to be a sheet of stationary wedged between the door and the door frame.

Brady watched as Ben read the note, then reread it, and then reread it a third time.

"Not bad news, I hope," Brady said.

"Some kind of prank, I guess," Ben replied, and handed the note to Brady.

Brady read out loud:

"Two of our martyrs have been lost in the jihad against the Great Satan. Their deaths will be avenged."

"Begorra and Blessed Mary," Brady said. "This is not good."

"Probably just someone trying to be funny," Ben said. "You don't take this seriously do you?"

"Well now first of all, not many people know of your involvement with any of the events of the past few weeks. We have pretty much kept your name out of it. But does it strike you as odd that the note mentions only two martyrs? Not three, but two."

Ben thought a moment before replying. "We thought we had all three of the terrorists. Sawyer, Sanchez and Suzie. Al Khafi, Mullah and Fatima. But I've always thought that Sanchez didn't fit the profile of a religious fanatic. More like your opportunist crook. You don't suppose that he was just a business partner of the terrorists? Someone they used to get explosives and guns or whatever they needed. You think there's a chance that the third terrorist is still out there?"

"I think you've hit the proverbial nail on the head," Brady said. "Right you are about Sanchez. Sweet Mary and I should have seen it before. Mullah is still loose, and now looking for revenge. I'm calling this in to my office right now. And you will be locking all of the doors and pulling the shades. We'll not be taking any chances here."

Ben did as Brady said, then studied the note once again. It was typed on a plain sheet of paper, probably by a computer printer. There was nothing out of the ordinary about it—the kind that you would find at any office store. The note was unsigned.

"Well now the situation has changed just a wee bit," Brady announced as he closed his cell phone and replaced it in the holder on his belt. "I'm no longer your guest and I'm no longer on sick leave. Back on active duty with an assignment to protect you from the bad guys. That means I am in charge and you will follow my orders. The company wants me to send the note to them, but I doubt they will be getting anything out of it except our finger prints. In the meantime it's a low profile we'll be keeping."

"Oh boy," Ben said. "Last time you came here to protect me, as I recall, we ended up in a shoot out. Think you could manage to keep it a little simpler this time?"

"Aye, I think I might. Our terrorist doesn't have access to all of Sanchez's gang of cutthroats this time around. We'll probably be faced with a one-on-one situation. Or two-on-one since you have me."

"Well, in that case, I am greatly relieved."

* * * * *

Several days later Ben was becoming increasingly restless. Being confined to his house was not anything that sat well with a man who was used to roaming the hills in the great outdoors. Especially at this time of year when the aspen were a brilliant yellow and orange.

"Brady, I've got to make a trip to our local supermarket and get some groceries. We're about out of everything."

"Oh no you don't, my fine feathered friend. You're not stepping foot outside of this house until we know more about this threatening letter of yours. And I can't go running to the store and leave you behind. Isn't there someone you know who would be only too glad to do a little shopping for you? Maybe you could call Ann up in Denver and have her come down and take care of us."

"I'm not getting her involved in any of this. Last thing we'd need is to have her around to get shot at or worse."

Just then Ben's phone rang

"That's probably her right now," Brady said. "Knew you needed help and called."

Ben picked up the phone. "Hello," he said, then listened closely to the voice on the other side of the line.

"This is Nadir Mullah Hassen," the voice said. "It is imperative that we talk. Meet me at the Pike's Peak coffee shop in Woodland Park in one hour. And do not call the police or bring your FBI friend with you. Do you understand?"

"Yes, I understand," Ben replied. "You're Mullah, the third terrorist. And just what do we have to talk about?" But the line had gone dead.

"He just wants to meet and have a conservation," Ben said. "At a coffee shop in town in 60 minutes."

"You'll not be going," Brady said. "He wants to get you out in the open. We'll have to stand him up, and then see where that leads us."

"But he wants to talk. This may be our chance to learn who he is and what he wants."

"We already know what he wants—to kill you. Remember? Revenge, I think he said."

"Look, Brady, I'm not sitting around like a prisoner in my own house any longer. If there's a chance that this could lead us somewhere, then I'm going. Period. Final statement. No arguing."

Brady sighed. "Then I'll be coming along. I'll watch from across the street. And you'll be taking one of your revolvers in that oversized pocket in your winter coat. If there is any funny business you may be needing it."

CHAPTER SIXTEEN

Ben arrived at the coffee shop a few minutes early, ordered a cup of coffee, and took a chair at a table near the front of the shop. He looked across the street at the Ben Franklin variety store, but could see no sign of Brady, who had driven in 15 minutes earlier in Ben's pick up truck.

Ben studied the people who were in the shop. At a table half way back sat a small man with a shiny bald head, but with heavy sideburns on the side. He had a narrow bird-like face marked by thick glasses through which he was reading the news in the local paper. Across from him there was a rather large woman, judging by the bulk pushing out from the inside of her winter coat. Her hair was untidy and her face without make-up. She grasped a latte in her thick fingers as she glanced around the room.

Another lady sat behind her with a baby stroller. Ben couldn't see the little one beneath the heap of blankets. The woman was probably in her twenties, or early thirties, and although not exactly pretty was still not unattractive. A young couple sat across from her, obviously absorbed in each other. *They've got other things on their minds besides terrorism*, Ben thought.

He sipped his coffee slowly, as other people arrived and left. The mouse-like man with the thick glasses was the first to leave, then the heavy woman. Followed by the young couple, and finally the woman with the baby carriage. Others took their place, drank their coffee, and left. Twenty minutes went by, then thirty, but no one approached him. An hour later Ben accepted the fact that Mullah wasn't going to show up. He was just getting up from the table when his cell phone rang.

"I told you to come alone," the voice said. "Do you not think I saw your FBI friend across the street? Now we will have to take other measures." The line went dead.

Ben walked out of the shop, and Brady came out of the store across the street. "Looks like we blew it," Ben said. "He spotted you across the street. Pretty good trick since I couldn't see you myself."

"Probably saw me when I first got there," Brady said. "Well, it's back to the old waiting game then." After a moment he added, "I guess as long as we're in town we might as well do that shopping you wanted. If he had wanted to do anything here he could have done it already."

As they entered the grocery store Brady remarked, "You know what I'd like that we're out of are those frozen cinnamon rolls. And some more green chili peppers. Two things we never had in good old Ireland when I was a wee one."

Ben smiled at Brady's exuberance. He wished he could feel the same.

* * * * *

Several more days went by with no word from Mullah. Then they got a call from a frantic Donald. The words poured out rapidly.

"Ben, Ann's missing. Nobody knows where she is. We were supposed to have lunch together at noon, but she didn't show up and nobody knows where she is. The police can't decide if she's really missing or if this is just another case of a woman ditching an unwanted boy friend. You've got to have Brady call them."

"Whoa. Slow down. Have you called her on her cell phone?"

"Yes. A dozen times. There is no answer. She went to a church women's group meeting this morning, and left there around 11:30. She was supposed to meet me here at La Baguette, but hasn't shown up. I've called her home and cell phones over and over but nobody answers. She told people at the meeting that she was meeting me for lunch, so I know she hasn't forgotten or anything like that. Have Brady call the Denver police—here—this is the number—303-398-6422, and ask for a Sergeant Kirby."

Ben handed the phone to Brady without speaking. *Ann— missing? Where could she be? What could have happened?* His mind ran through a dozen possibilities of why she might have missed the luncheon date.

After listening to Donald's frantic words, Brady called the Sergeant, identified himself, and assured him that Mr. Klein was a dependable, rational person, and that Mrs. Ann Hopkins was a responsible woman who would not have disappeared without some very good reason.

When he finished Ben said, "We've got to get up to Denver. Find out what happened." Then, after a pause, "You don't think this could be related to any of this threatening stuff I've been getting, do you?"

"One wrong and one right," Brady replied. "No, you're not going to Denver, and yes, I think this might very well be related to our Mr. Mullah. It's not pessimistic that I am, but we can't rule out the possibility. And if it is, and Mullah wants to contact us, he'll do it here, not in Denver. Besides, there's absolutely nothing we can do there."

Ben realized Brady was right, but he was a man used to being in the forefront of things. Sitting around doing nothing—just waiting—was the hardest thing in the world for him to do. That had been the part of Mary's illness that had been almost unbearable for him.

"Nothing to do but wait then," Brady said, as if he had read Ben's thoughts.

Ben thought a moment, and then reluctantly accepted Brady's assessment. He walked over to the entertainment center, selected a CD by Tony Bennett, inserted it into the disc player, then strolled over to the sliding doors to the back patio and looked out. The snow was starting to fall heavily. The weatherman had warned on the morning news that the first major snow storm of the winter was going to hit over the next two days. Eight to ten inches of the white powdery stuff was being predicted. Ben loved the snow, but at the moment was not in a mood to appreciate anything. The thought that Ann's disappearance might be connected to his own troubles disturbed him, and made him feel that he was responsible. He prayed that she would show up unharmed and that this had nothing to do with his own Mr. Mullah.

Another day went by, and no word of Ann. The Denver police were now investigating the case seriously, interviewing the ladies from the Church women's group, quizzing Donald in great depth, and had even had a telephone interview with Ben and Brady. So far they had not been able to turn up anything.

The snow continued to fall. Drifts three feet deep were piling up on the back porch. Ben worked off some of his energy shoveling the snow from the walk in front of the house. Then he got the snow blower out of the garage and cleared the driveway out to the county road.

THE THIRD MUSKETEER

Around noon Donald called and said the police had found Ann's car at a Walgreen's parking lot. It seemed that she had picked up a prescription there around 11:45 on the day she was to have met Donald for lunch. This news further dampened Ben's spirits.

Then Mullah called again.

"We were to have met in a public place for our little chat," the voice on the other end said. "Alone. But you had to bring along your FBI friend, which I specifically asked you not to do. Now the rules have changed. I am inviting not only yourself for our short meeting, but also your lady friend, who incidentally is already in my company. Would you like to talk to her?"

Before Ben could reply Ann was on the phone. "Ben, I'm all right. This guy is crazy. Don't trust anything he says."

There was the sound of a sharp slap and a muffled cry from Ann, and Mullah returned to the phone. "I presume you have heard enough to know that I am serious about our little get together. Just the three of us, and nobody gets hurt. If your FBI friend shows up anywhere in the vicinity, I can't be responsible for what might happen to your friend here. Understood?"

"Understood," Ben replied.

"Fine. Meet us at the Summerhaven camp ground, just north of Woodland Park, in 45 minutes. At the camp table nearest the entrance."

"You can't be serious," Ben said. "That place is closed for the winter. You can't drive into it. And have you looked outside lately? We're in the middle of a blizzard. You can't see five feet in front of you."

"Your station wagon has four wheel drive as I recall, so you should have no trouble getting there. You can park on the highway and walk in," Mullah said. "You will find your lady friend there, alive or dead. It's up to you. Forty-five minutes." The phone went dead.

Ben had turned the speaker phone on as soon as he realized it was Mullah on the other end. Now he looked at Brady who had been listening intently.

"You can't go," Brady said. "It's all a set-up to get you out in the open so he can kill you."

"You heard him," Ben replied. "He just wants to talk. If he wanted to kill me why didn't he do it at the coffee shop?"

"Ben, he had no intention of meeting you there. He probably knew I would be tagging along, but it wouldn't have made any difference one way or the other. He wasn't going to show. All of that was just a prelude for this. To get you in an isolated place where he could finish the job with no witnesses and no interference."

"I guess it doesn't matter," Ben said. "He has Ann, and I am responsible. I don't have any choice but to do as he says. Maybe he will let her go if he has me."

Brady sighed. "He won't. But I understand. He's holding all the cards. Tell me about this camp site."

"It's several miles north of town on Highway 67. There's no way to circle around and come down from the north. So he'll probably be somewhere south of the park entrance waiting for me to drive past and to make sure nobody—like yourself—is following. Probably there already to make sure you don't go ahead of me. He seems to know I have a Subaru and a Ford truck so he'll be watching out for them."

"Well, me lad, here's what we'll do," Brady said.

CHAPTER SEVENTEEN

Ben leaned forward in the seat of his Subaru, trying to see the road ahead of him in the blinding snow. The flakes were melting as they landed on the window, but then froze on the glass, making his windshield wipers ineffective. Every several miles Ben had to stop the car, get out and scrape the ice off, before proceeding. He had met no other cars going north out of town, and only one car going the other way. A snow plow had cleared the road not too long before, but it was already covered again from the blowing white crystals.

At last he saw the highway sign, now nearly covered with freezing snow, which read "Summerhaven Camp Grounds." There was a chain link barrier across the road leading to the campground with a "Closed" sign hanging from it.

Ben parked the car and climbed out. There was no sign of tire tracks anywhere, or footprints leading off the road. He wore a heavy parka with a hood which he pulled down over his head, and dark sun glasses to cut the glare of the snow. His hands were covered with thin leather gloves, which he stuck deep into the side pockets of his coat to keep them warm as he began to trudge through the snow to the camp area. He felt somewhat encouraged as he gripped the handle of his favorite revolver in the deep pocket of the jacket, a Taurus .357 magnum single action pistol he used when hunting small game. Fifteen minutes later he was at the table Mullah had indicated, but there was no sign of life or evidence that anyone had been around since the storm had started the previous day. The snow didn't let up.

Ben waited for what seemed an eternity, moving around and stomping his feet to keep warm. Perhaps half an hour went by with no sound but that of the blowing wind, and nothing visible more than 30 feet away. Then he thought he heard a motor in the distance, the sound fading in and out with the cross currents of the blizzard. As the reverberations grew louder and more pronounced Ben realized it was a snow sled coming from the south, paralleling the highway.

He peered through the blanket of snow masking the horizon, and finally was able to make it out, now only 30 feet away, approaching slowly. There were two people on it. The driver was wearing a heavy red parka; the hood pulled low over his head and dark snow glasses masking his face. Behind him sat another figure with a heavy blanket over his or her head and wrapped tightly around the body. Ben could not make out who it was, but presumed it must be Ann.

The sled came to a stop 20 feet in front of Ben. Ben clutched the revolver in his pocket, while the driver rose and slowly stepped off the sled. He stared at Ben for a few minutes before bending back over the toboggan, pulling a semi-automatic rifle from the floor. Before Ben could react the gun was pointed directly at Ben's midsection, and Ben realized with a sinking feeling that he had lost the initiative.

Mullah backed away from the snow sled, keeping the rifle trained on Ben. "There is a knife on the floor of the sled," he said. "I'm afraid it was necessary to tie your friend here onto the sled. She has been most uncooperative. You may cut her bonds now and let her get out."

Ben approached the snowmobile. Ann was peering out of the blanket wrapped tightly around her. "Oh, Ben. I'm so sorry. You shouldn't have come. I think he will kill us both."

"No need to worry, Ann," Ben replied. "I have his word that he will let you go."

Ben cut Ann loose and helped her from the sled. She had no hat, and was wearing only a light weight coat. She was shivering uncontrollably. He turned to Mullah and very slowly reached into his coat pocket and withdrew his car keys. Mullah watched him closely, the gun never wavering from Ben's chest.

Ben recognized him now as the man he had seen in the coffee shop a few days ago. The one who was bald headed, and who wore thick glasses.

Ben turned back to Ann. "Here are the keys to my wagon," he said. "It's down on the main road. Go on down there, start the car and get warmed up. I'll be along shortly as soon as Mullah and I have our little talk." Ann stared at him. They both knew they were not apt to get out of this alive.

"I'm afraid that won't be possible," Mullah said. "I need your lady friend to hang around for a little longer."

Ben turned back to Mullah. "You promised that she wouldn't be harmed. Let her go and then we can talk."

"One of the things I especially like about our leader, Muhammad, is that he has said it is permissible to lie to infidels when it is necessary. I'm afraid this is one of those times, and that I might have told a minor untruth when talking with you. In point of fact, I have very little to say to you, except to let you know that I intend to avenge the death of Fatima."

As Mullah talked Ben removed his gloves and handed them to Ann to put on. He then thrust both hands into the pockets of his coat, wrapping his right hand around the handle of the gun.

"You will remove your hands from your pockets," Mullah said, "and keep them at all times where I can see them."

Ben hesitated, trying to decide if now was the time to take a chance. But the semi-automatic was pointed directly at his chest, and the safety was still set on his revolver. By time he switched the safety off and tried to aim and shoot through his coat Mullah could have five bullets into his body. With great misgivings he released his grip on the weapon and pulled his hands out of the jacket.

"You see," Mullah continued, "Fatima was not only a comrade, but my lover. She was a woman I greatly admired, and you were the instrument of her death. So now, Ben Foxworth, it is your turn. I will concentrate on Mr. Brady Jones, later. But before you meet Allah, you will see your lady die. I want you to know and experience the pain and agony I have felt over these past weeks when someone close meets an unexpected and inappropriate death." Mullah turned the rifle from Ben and aimed directly at Ann.

Ben gave Ann a hard push with his left hand and sent her sprawling to the ground just as Mullah's rifle thundered in the silence. At the same time the sound of another gun being fired could be heard, and Mullah spun half around, falling back into the snow, a pool of bright red blood forming underneath his body.

For a moment everything seemed frozen in time, and then Ann pushed herself up to a sitting position in the snow. "W— What just happened?" she said.

"I think," Ben replied, "that our Irish friend just saved our lives."

Ann saw that Ben was staring off to the right. She turned to see a figure through the blinding snow struggling towards them on snowshoes, clutching a rifle in both hands. It was Brady.

"But how.... Where did he come from?" Ann said. "Mullah watched the road carefully. The only car that went through was the snow plow, and nobody followed you. We waited half an hour to make sure of that."

"You just said it," Ben said. "The snowplow. Brady was laying on the floor when it went past, and then the driver let him off after the next turn. He made his way back here on those snowshoes."

As Brady came up to the two Ben said, "Man, you sure took your time. Where in the world have you been? I thought you were never going to show up."

Brady glared at Ben for a few seconds before replying. "Sure and by the Sweet Mary you told me that walking in these blasted fish nets was like flying through the woods. I almost gave up several times. If it hadn't been for my great strength and perseverance you would have become a mere footnote on my resume."

Ben felt a deep laugh build in his abdomen, more from relief than from humor at Brady's remarks. Ann, still sitting in the snow, also started giggling uncontrollably, and Brady grinned broadly at the both of them.

Finally Ben said, "Well—are we just going to stand around here in this blizzard and freeze to death, or are we going home."

"I vote for home," Ann said.

Ben helped Ann to her feet, and with his arm around her, the three of them trudged back to the Outback.

EPILOGUE

The snow was falling softly in the small graveyard high in the mountains, decorating the tombstones and memorials with a crown of icy, majestic splendor. At one of the sites a dozen red roses lay on the mound, their color accentuated by the carpet of white snow on which they lay, with more falling from the sky and gently covering them.

A man stood beside the grave, dressed warmly in a dark green, down jacket and wearing a cap with ear flaps pulled down tightly about his head.

"So that's what happened at the class reunion, Mary," Ben was saying. "You were always nagging me to go to one of them. Said it might be kind of exciting, as I recall. Well, it certainly was that. And thanks for the warning to be careful."

"It was great to reestablish friendships with my old high school friends, even if it ended abruptly. We used to call ourselves the Three Musketeers, and for a short time there that's who we were once again. 'One for all and all for one.' I am happy that I went. I feel like it enriched my life, and I probably wouldn't have gone if it hadn't been for you."

"I guess I must be getting old. Like everyone else that has reached this age I look back at the times when we were growing up and think of them as the 'good old days.' A time when life was simpler, the pace slower, and there were no gangs, drugs or cell phones. We considered ourselves a Christian nation, although our current leader tells us that this is no longer true. I think we knew who we were and where we were going, something I'm not sure young people are blessed with today. But we can never go back. We're in a different time and place in our civilization's journey."

"Beth is still after me to sell the place and move to Seattle. It would be nice being nearer the grandkids, but to tell you the truth I'd be like a fish out of water if I ever left here. Maybe someday when I'm old and decrepit, but I'm not there yet."

"As a matter of fact, I have just accepted a teaching job with the Mountaineer College in the Springs to lecture on Business Law three days a week. That ought to keep me out of trouble and my mind active for a while."

"I confess I don't know what to think of Islam—a word I hardly knew when we were young. I know that many of their values are similar to ours. Obedience to God, kindness, consideration for others."

"But the trouble is we have two faces of Islam, and one of them has sworn to destroy us and establish Shari'ah law, the fundamental law of Islam, throughout the land. They foster terrorism, hate and intolerance, while the other Islam denounces their actions and pray for peace."

"The problem for most of us is how to be at war with the one who fights in the name of Islam and not be somewhat suspicious of the other who strongly embraces the same religion. Especially when they set themselves apart from the rest of society by their dress and customs and insist that we adapt to their religious requirements."

"I guess as I said, I'm getting too old and set in my ways to keep up with the changing world."

Ben leaned over, picked up the roses, shook off the fresh snow, and gently laid them back on the grave.

"Saturday, I'm going to Denver for dinner at Ann's. Donald will be there, too. The three of us have become good friends. Donald's a little on the stuffy side, but a decent guy. Next month I'm heading back to Philadelphia to stand up with Brady at his wedding. He and Sara, his fiancée, are wonderful people. You would love them. I think their marriage will be perfect, since they both realize it is something that they will have to work on everyday and never take it for granted."

"I have a new four-legged friend that keeps me company on these cold winter nights. I've named her Lady. You would like her also. I know you were always partial to Golden Retrievers. She is beautiful—long golden hair—a wonderful disposition—and obeys me without question, whenever I give her a command. I found her at the dog adoption agency, down in the Springs. Seemed she belonged to an elderly man that was moving into a nursing home and had to give her up. I can imagine, it must have broken his heart."

Ben glanced up at the darkening sky. "Well, guess I'd better be on my way. It's getting dark early these days. Looks like it will be a cold and wet winter."

Ben turned and trudged through the snow, back to the road and to his station wagon. In a few minutes, he was out of sight and silence descended once again on the soft winter scene.